BADMAN'S HOLIDAY

Center Point
Large Print

**This Large Print Book carries the
Seal of Approval of N.A.V.H.**

BADMAN'S HOLIDAY

Will Cook

Center Point Publishing
Thorndike, Maine

This Center Point Large Print edition
is published in the year 2005 by arrangement with
Golden West Literary Agency.

Copyright © 1958 by Will Cook.
Copyright © renewed 1986 by Theola G. Cook-Lewis.

The text of this Large Print edition is unabridged. In other
aspects, this book may vary from the original edition. Printed in
Thailand. Set in 16-point Times New Roman type.

ISBN 1-58547-583-1

Library of Congress Cataloging-in-Publication Data

Cook, Will.
    Badman's holiday / Will Cook.--Center Point large print ed.
        p. cm.
    ISBN 1-58547-583-1 (lib. bdg. : alk. paper)
    1. Large type books. I. Title.

PS3553.O5547B33 2005
813'.54--dc22

2004027197

BADMAN'S HOLIDAY

AFTER ELEVEN YEARS' RESIDENCE IN TWO PINES, Lincoln McKeever had grown accustomed to a life of quiet boredom, and during his three and a half years as sheriff, McKeever had now and then been irritated by the deadly monotony, for all infractions of the law were petty, and the West's wildness seemed to circumvent Two Pines. McKeever suspected that this was because Two Pines lacked allure, the easy-money kind that drew the toughs and the gunmen and the card sharks. Or perhaps the people of Two Pines had something to do with this serenity; they were so settled in dull routine that life had anesthetized itself, and moved only in the rut of habit.

The trouble with Two Pines, McKeever decided, was that there was too much of a good thing there. No one really had to hustle for anything; the challenge was gone. Why, there hadn't been a new business established in seven years. People went on working, making about the same wages, spending about the same, saying what they had always said, thinking what they had always thought. And I'm as bad as the next guy, McKeever thought.

Unlike most towns, Two Pines did not depend on any one thing for its revenue. To the south was the cattle country, good graze, plenty of water, and the men who worked the land were "stayers," even the working hands. McKeever had roamed enough to know men who followed cattle. Loose-footed usually, always quitting, moving, hiring on someplace else—but not around Two Pines. They just seemed to fit in, coming to town every Saturday night, having their drink, playing a few hands of cards, making no fuss. McKeever always watched them, for they'd stand around on the street corners, talking about the weather or cattle, the things they already knew about, week after week; and McKeever wondered when they'd break, do something different, maybe something illegal, just to be doing it.

But this never happened.

To the north was the timber. McKeever had originally come to Two Pines to work in the woods, but he'd stayed on as sheriff even when his good sense told him to go someplace else. Logging was good. Not spectacular, but there were a hundred years of it if a man held himself back and didn't get greedy and cut it all down in the first ten years. And they held back, taking it out slow and enticing the weekly-pay, bread-and-butter-on-the-table kind of logger to stay on.

These men were another concern for Lincoln McKeever, for he knew the breed—tough, and mean sometimes, a pot of trouble just waiting for an excuse to boil over. Only it never did. Saturday nights they'd come into town, walk up and down the streets, talk, loaf, buy in the stores, then go home. Now and then there would be a fist fight, but it never went any farther. At one time, a few of the sporting bloods rode over to Woodland, a neighboring town, to let off a little of the hell that is in all men, but McKeever noticed that they soon stopped this. The ride was long and it was a lot of trouble for nothing, so they stayed in Two Pines, leaning against the same lampposts week after week, talking to the same men about the same things, and doing the same work day after day.

Logging and cattle—two fine, stable industries that had never mixed, but in Two Pines they did, as though it were too much trouble to fight. Still there was more, to the west—the galena mines. Through Two Pines came the long ore wagons hauling the stuff to the smelters to be fired down into lead pigs; there they were shipped eighty miles overland to the railroad. McKeever had been in boom camps; he knew miners and teamsters and during his first year in office he had kept an eye constantly on them, especially on Saturday nights, but he was wasting his time.

The miners had their saloon, the cattlemen had theirs, and the loggers liked a place on the edge of town. Even McKeever's routine was well established. He sat on the hotel porch each Saturday evening until seven, then he made his rounds. His first stop was The Palace, the cattleman's place. The four "big" men had their poker game going; same table, and about the same level of win or lose. Now and then fresh blood would be invited to enter, but not often; people in Two Pines wiggled and worked until things were just right, then worked harder to keep them that way. At the cattleman's place, the drinking men would be drinking, the talking men talking, and the listeners listening; this never varied, and Joel Lovering, who ran The Palace, knew what his Saturday night take would be even before the first of the hands drifted into the place. Now and then the sameness of it all would get someone down and he would look for something to change, something small, like the color of a man's eye.

These minor fights were no problem to McKeever, who broke them up and let it go at that.

At the miners' pace, a man ran into a little of the old country, Welsh songs, rough Irish jokes, and men who liked to bear-wrestle; the events started at seven-thirty and McKeever watched them in case someone lost his temper.

For a man just turning thirty, Lincoln McKeever figured that he had most of his troubles behind him, and it was a satisfying thought. McKeever was long and lanky, with a shock of unruly hair that hung in a lock beneath the sweatband of his hat. He moved slowly, talked slowly, and some people had once made the mistake of thinking that his mind worked at that pace. But those men were now in jail, with eleven more years to go before their sentence was up.

Twice, after he had been elected sheriff, two strangers passing through had made the fatal mistake of believing that because McKeever carried his pistol in his coat pocket he would be clumsy at it. They were buried, at township expense and only Mrs. Moody, who thought about those things, placed flowers on their graves each Easter.

THE sun finally slid behind the hills and this announced McKeever's supper hour; he walked a block west to the Hanover House and took his usual table next to the door. He did not order, for years of eating here had established his likes and dislikes as firmly as anyone else in Two Pines. McKeever could look out the window and see the main street, or a good part of it. Everyone was in his place, like actors waiting for the first curtain to go up. One of these days, he thought, someone is going to forget what he always says or does, and then there'll be hell to pay.

Between his apple pie and his coffee there was a lull of several minutes during which Lincoln McKeever kept looking toward the door, and when a heavy, bluff-faced man came in. McKeever smiled and toed a chair away from the table.

"Don't you ever eat anything but apple pie?" the man said, sitting down. He put his hat on a vacant chair, then signaled the waiter to bring his cup of coffee.

"I could set my watch by the time you come through that door," McKeever said softly. "You want to do me a favor, Finley?"

"What kind?"

McKeever smiled. "The next time you buy a new coat, make it something else besides brown corduroy."

"I like brown corduroy," Finley Fineen said. Then he laughed. "Lincoln, suppose I bought blue serge. Do you know what would happen? No one in town would know me. Man, you don't think that they look at your face any more, do you? You see a straw hat walk past, that's Huddlemyer, the butcher. He's worn straw hats since anyone can remember. You see a parasol and it's Richardson at the bank; he carries the damn thing during August dog days, when it hasn't rained in thirty-one years in August." Fineen shook his head, a bit sadly. "We've got to stay the same, Lincoln. Lord, if anyone changed it would upset the whole damned township." Then he shrugged. "I'm too lazy to scratch anyway. The lead mine ordered four new wagons this afternoon. A nice profit there." His coffee came and he softened its heat with water. "Poker game tonight, Lincoln?"

"You ask that every Saturday," McKeever said. "Finley, don't we always play poker?"

Fineen laughed. "Yeah. But I guess I keep hoping you'll shock me and say to hell with it, just to be different."

"If it bores you, then cut it out."

"Bores me? My God, this whole damned town bores me." He drank some of his coffee. "Ah, what difference does it make? If we weren't playing poker, it would be something else. Don't you get tired of one day following another, with tomorrow so damned predictable?"

"No," McKeever said. "I like Two Pines, Finley. I kicked around for a long time; my father was a restless man. It's good to find a rut that fits." A rumble rattled dishes in the kitchen and McKeever raised his head. "That thunder?"

"Yeah, it was clouding up," Fineen said. "Damn, I hope it doesn't start to rain. I've got some oak outside that I want kept dry."

"It sometimes rains on Saturday nights," McKeever said.

The hotel clerk came into the dining room, had a quick look, then went out to stand on the porch, peering up at the dark sky. Fineen studied the man briefly. "You know what he'll say when I leave?"

McKeever nodded. "Looks like we're going to have some rain after all."

"That's it exactly," Fineen said. "You know something, if he says that to me I think I'll hit him."

"Better not," McKeever said gently, but the warning was there. "Finley, a man's what he wants to be. If you want them to talk about something different, go out in the middle of the street and take your pants off."

"To hell with you," Fineen said, smiling. "Around nine?"

"With the usual boring punctuality," McKeever said.

Fineen went out, pausing in the doorway to look back; McKeever was having his coffee. The clerk, still on the porch, turned and said, "Looks like we're going to have some rain after all, Mr. Fineen."

"Samson, you're an alert bastard," Fineen said then walked on down the street. He was a tall man, over two hundred pounds, and muscled by twenty years of blacksmithing and carriage-making. There were some people in Two Pines who thought a man with Fineen's money ought to quit manual labor and spend his time behind a cloud of expensive cigar smoke, with his feet elevated to a desk, but Fineen's habits were too well set to be broken.

HE stopped at the drugstore, then stood on the porch

as the first spatter of rain dimpled the street's dust. Then he went inside and into the back room where Bill Daley sniffed with his eternal head cold. He packaged medicines that cured others, but not himself.

Daley was thin, almost sickly in both physique and complexion. He had thin red hair and a nose reddened by constant blowing. He looked around when Fineen stopped in the doorway.

"It's beginning to rain," Fineen said.

Daley looked at him for a moment, then said, "You know, if you hadn't come along, Finley, I'd never have been able to have figured that out for myself."

"All right, all right," Fineen said. "I'm going over to the office. You be over in half an hour?"

"I always am," Daley said. "My wife's over to Bertha Mailer's gossiping as usual, and my help is dipping their fingers into the till, as usual. As usual, I'll be there in a half hour. Wade Stanton too?"

"Of course," Fineen said. "Bring the stuff."

"What? Tonight?" Daley spoke sharply, with a touch of apprehension.

"It's raining, isn't it?"

Fineen walked out and down the street, not stopping until he came to his office. His mill and carriage yard was behind the main building; he unlocked the door and went into the back room, there turning up the lamp he had left faintly burning.

The rain was coming down steadily now, drumming on the roof, turning his yard into one big mud puddle. He listened to the rain, then smiled and went across the compound to his small machine shop where he made carriage parts. A huge screw press sat in one corner, and in the darkness he disassembled the handle, a six-foot length of steel pipe. Taking this into the office, he locked the back door and the front door, and then went to his desk. From the bottom drawer he took a walnut stock and fitted the pipe to it, but before he fastened it securely he took out a steel gunlock and screwed it onto the pipe. With this seated into the stock, he locked the two small wing clamps and set the thing in the corner.

Someone knocked on the front door and Fineen opened it. Wade Stanton stepped inside and flogged water from his wide-brimmed hat. He was cattle, from boots to hat, thirty-some and wealthy enough to have considerable say in Two Pines. "Have you seen Daley?" Stanton asked.

"He'll be here," Fineen said. "Come on in the back."

Stanton followed him and Fineen closed the separating door. Stanton's eyes went to the gun in the corner. "That's an ugly thing," he said.

"It'll do the job," Fineen said casually.

Stanton turned and looked at him. "This doesn't bother you at all, does it, Finley?"

"No. Does it you?"

Stanton shook his head. "No, we've gone over it so many times that I wake up at night believing it's already been done." He put his hands in his pockets. "Where's Lincoln McKeever?"

"Now, you know where he is," Fineen said. "He's over to the teamsters' saloon watching them knock bottles off the bar with a bull whip. You ought to get around this town, Wade. See what's going on."

"I know what's going on," Stanton said sourly. "Nothing's going on around this damned town. I get sick of doing nothing. I've thought about staying home one of these Saturday nights just to listen to the speculation on why I didn't come to town."

"Habit can be a blessing," Fineen said. He cocked his head to one side. "That'll be Bill Daley." He went to the front again and came back with the druggist. Daley and Stanton looked at each other, then Fineen motioned for them to sit down.

"We've got an hour," he said. "Relax." His glance touched Daley. "Let me have it."

DALEY took a package from under his coat and laid it on Fineen's desk. After unwrapping it, Fineen said, "You sure this will go off?" He turned the small brass projectile over, examining it carefully.

"Damned sure," Daley said. "Finley, it'll kill the horse. Blow him to hell and gone."

"But will it make smoke?"

Daley nodded. "Like a choked-off brush fire."

"That's good," Fineen said. "Everything going on as usual out there?" He nodded toward the street.

"The rain doesn't change much," Daley said.

"All right," Fineen said. "Now let's go over the whole thing again, from top to bottom."

"Hell, we've been over it a hundred times," Stanton said.

"We'll go over it once more," Fineen said, not

arguing. "Dalridge will leave town at eight-thirty, as usual."

"We hope," Daley said.

Fineen's expression mirrored his impatience. "He has for the past year and a half, and that's good enough for me. Look, he can't help but do what he always does. He'll take the south road." Fineen laughed. "Last time he took the lane out by Miles' place. This time it's the south road. A while ago I was talking to Lincoln McKeever about us—you know, being creatures of habit. This whole thing is based on habit. The habits of all of us. Now you take Dalridge, he's been taking the mine's money to the railhead for nearly four years, and I'll bet he'd swear that he's never established a pattern. Yet he has, for in spite of his taking different roads, he's developed a sequence. I believe we can predict where he'll be tonight at twenty minutes to nine."

"We've waited long enough for rain," Stanton said. "Especially rain on an alternate Saturday night."

"Well, we've got rain tonight," Fineen said. "There's no better cover than a rainy night. We all agreed to that."

"What about McKeever?" Daley asked. "What if he comes early?"

"Has he ever come before nine in the last four years?"

"No," Daley said, "but he could—"

Fineen shook his head. "Gentlemen, we've agreed to use logic, haven't we? All right, then, let's stick to the plan. McKeever knows that our poker game starts at eight and he always comes in at nine, with Doc Harris. We'll take twenty-eight minutes to do the job and get back here. All right?"

"I'm sold," Stanton said. "I see no flaw in it, Finley."

"There isn't any flaw," Fineen said. "We'll take Dalridge on the south road because it's close to town. We'll bring the money back here, split it as we planned, then sit on it for five years. After that, we can mix it in with our spending and no one will ever know the difference." Fineen leaned back in his chair. "I think we all agree that criminals are caught trying to flee the scene of their crime. We won't flee at all." He spread his hands. "A man steals because he wants money. None of us needs money, we have plenty already. I'll bet McKeever drives himself ragged looking for the robbers, and all the time we'll be laughing at him."

"Not out loud," Stanton said. He got up and walked around the office. "You know, I get so goddamn bored, the same thing all the time, the same talk." He laughed. "I wonder if you know how much I've been looking forward to this just because it'll be different." He made a sweeping motion with his hand. "I've thought a lot about robbery since we first talked about this. This is different than just deciding to stick up the stage or something. Kind of a work of art, like a painting, or a poem."

"I like the idea of the money," Bill Daley said, sniffing. "This'll be the first dollar I've had in fifteen years that my wife won't get her hands on first. I'd like to go to St. Louis and—"

"None of that!" Fineen said sharply. "Damn it, this will work only if we stay here and keep our cover. Understand that, Daley?"

"Yeah, yeah, I understand it. I was only wishing, that's all."

"This is one time when you're not permitted to wish," Fineen said. "Bill, this will work if we stick to our cover. But the minute one of us breaks away from our usual routine, we'll draw suspicion like—"

We know that," Stanton said irritably. "Finley, how much do you suppose Dalridge will be carrying this time?"

"Close to sixty thousand," Fineen said. "It'll take that much to cover their subcontracts, teamsters, supplies, and all. I make it that they'll take nearly sixty thousand out of that vault." He laughed. "This way is better than going out to the mine and blowing it open, isn't it?"

"I never liked hard work anyway," Stanton said.

Finley Fineen consulted his watch. "Two minutes. Dalridge is halfway to town by now." He picked up his hat, then took three slickers from a closet; they slipped into them. From his desk he took out three revolvers and made sure they were unloaded.

"Don't you trust us, Finley?" This was Stanton's question.

"There'll only be one shot fired," Fineen said, picking up the huge gun leaning in the corner. He inserted the cartridge Bill Daley had made, and the druggist grew nervous.

"Be careful of that, Finley."

"I'm always careful," Fineen said, and led the way into the muddy yard. He hitched a team to a light, covered buggy. Stanton drove while Fineen lay flat in back, a tarpaulin over him.

Stanton knew where he was going and took all the back roads to get there. He left town and drove for nearly a mile, then parked at the junction, where a back road ran into the main road to the railhead.

From under the tarp, Fineen said, "Be sure and let him pass, Wade. He won't be going fast."

"I know how to do it," Stanton said with annoyance in his voice.

Bill Daley began to cough and Fineen said, "For Christ's sake, cut that out. That's a dead giveaway."

Daley choked his coughing, then Wade Stanton spoke, excitement in his voice. "God, here he comes!"

"Get set!" Fineen said, and by feel he checked the mechanism of the homemade gun to see that it was set to fire.

A buggy and driver passed, nearly obscured by the rain; then Wade Stanton lashed the team into motion. He drove like a wild man, skidding back and forth across the road, then controlled them enough to pass Dalridge. Fineen was waiting, the long muzzle lifted over the rim of the rear wheel, and when Stanton pulled slightly past Dalridge's rig, Fineen fired.

2.

FINLEY FINEEN HAD BEEN RIGHT; THE ONE SHOT killed the horse, upset the buggy and broke both of Dalridge's legs when it toppled over on him. Stanton sawed the rig to a halt, made a wild U turn and drove back; Fineen was out of the back before the rig stopped.

They put on bandannas quickly and ran to the overturned buggy. Stanton searched for the money sacks, and found them. Bill Daley heard Dalridge groaning and bent over him, a mistake if he ever made one, for Dalridge snatched the bandanna away, recognizing Daley.

Stanton had the money. Fineen looked at Dalridge for a moment, then said, "Nothing to do now but kill him."

The thought frightened Bill Daley. "Finley, that wasn't in the plan!"

"You damned fool, the plan's changed! You going to do it or am I?"

"I—I couldn't do it," Daley said.

"What're you going to kill him with?" Stanton asked. "You unloaded the guns."

Finley Fineen hesitated an instant, then clubbed Dalridge across the head with the barrel of his gun. Daley watched, his expression frozen as Fineen's gun rose and fell; he sounded as if he were smashing honeydew melons on a brick walk. Then Daley turned away and threw up and Fineen put his gun away.

"Let's go," Fineen said. "We're a minute off schedule now." He looked at Daley, then slapped him hard. "Snap out of it!" He shoved the man into the buggy, then crawled back under the tarp as Stanton drove back toward town, again taking the side roads.

He used the back door to Fineen's carriage yard and parked the rig. Daley stood coughing and sniffing while Fineen unhitched the team and put them in the barn. Stanton was standing by the back door when Fineen motioned him inside.

They put their slickers away and Fineen said, "There's a mop in back, Bill. Clean up that water on the floor."

While Daley worked the swab over the floor, Fineen took the homemade gun apart and put the steel pipe back into the press. He disassembled the firing mechanism and put that away, then he took the three sacks of money from Stanton and dropped them into the bottom desk drawer.

Daley was through mopping and at Fineen's nod, he took his place at the table. Stanton was shuffling cards and dealing the first hand. "Here," Fineen said, handing each of them a cigar.

"I don't smoke," Daley said. "Bad for my health." He took a bottle of pills from his coat pocket and popped one into his mouth.

"Smoke that cigar," Fineen said. "When McKeever gets here, I want this room full of smoke."

"He's right," Stanton said. "It's always foggy in here when McKeever arrives."

Fineen took a sack of cigar butts from his desk and filled the two metal ashtrays. Then he threw the sack away. "Let's get some money on the table." He looked at his watch while they laid out coins and bills. "Don't divide it evenly," he snapped. "We've been playing poker for an hour, and who heard of three even winners." He gave most of the money to Daley and then picked up his cards.

"I'll never get that sound out of my mind," Bill Daley said softly. "His head just busted wide—"

"Shut your mouth!" Stanton snapped. "Finley did what he had to do."

"I know, but we didn't figure on murder."

Fineen looked up and his eyes were gray glass. "God damn you, Bill, don't crack on me. McKeever will be here in two minutes. You act the same as always."

"All right," Daley said. "But I'll have to work at it."

"Then work at it," Fineen said flatly. "You expect to get that money for nothing?" He made a fan of his cards and Stanton opened.

THE room was full of smoke when McKeever arrived. He shook his head and squinted at them, then pulled his chair aside and sat down. "Doc Harris will be along in a minute," he said. He looked at Daley's pile. "Are you winning?"

"It looks that way," Daley said, pausing to cough.

Fineen looked at McKeever. "Bill's luck has changed, Lincoln."

"I guess it has," McKeever said, smiling. "I was

counting on taking twenty or so off him tonight."

"Still raining?" Stanton asked.

"Just listen to it," McKeever said. "The creek'll be up when you go home, Wade."

Stanton shrugged. "My horse has long legs."

Everyone looked up when Doctor Harris came in, pipe going, water shedding off his coat. He put his hat and black bag aside, then draped his coat over the back of a chair before taking his place at the table. He was a dry-skinned little man who always squinted when he talked. Noticing Bill Daley's pile, Harris said, "You been eating meat, Bill?"

"Huh?"

"You're winning," Harris said. "That will spoil a beautiful friendship quicker than anything, Bill. What makes you such a delightful poker partner is that you consistently lose." He slapped the table. "Let's deal, huh?"

McKeever took his cards, made a modest bet after Harris opened, then said, "Good thing you don't have any house calls tonight, Doc."

"The hell I don't. Mrs. Ludlow's going to have another any time now. I left word that I was here." He nodded toward his bag. "Got my tools and everything."

"How's your wife?" McKeever asked.

Stanton looked up. "You talking to me?"

McKeever winked at Harris. "Now who else here has a wife young enough for me to be interested in?"

"If you want her," Stanton said flatly, "you can have her."

"Hey," Fineen said. "This started out to be a joke." His eyes warned Stanton. "What's got into you, anyway?"

"Nothing," Stanton said. "Betty gets on my nerves once in a while. We had a fight before I left for town tonight."

Harris squinted. "Wade, all husbands and wives fight. Didn't anyone ever tell you that?" He checked his hand. "How long have you been married now? A year?"

"Closer to two," Stanton said. "Hell, do we have to talk about it?"

"It was your topic," McKeever said. "Let me have three cards, Bill."

"What do you tell your wife when you lose at poker, Bill?" This was Harris' question, an irritating one, because they all knew that Daley never spoke to his wife unless she invited him to speak.

"Want to know something?" Daley asked. "One of these days she's going to say something to me and I'll beat her damned brains out!" He closed his mouth suddenly and looked stricken, his complexion chalky.

"What's the matter with you?" Harris asked, his professional interest aroused. "Taking too many of those damned patent pills? Or maybe you ought to take one now."

"I don't feel good," Bill Daley said lamely.

Finley Fineen said, "Hell, you're always sick or complaining. You're all right, Bill. You just keep telling yourself that."

"Sure," Daley said. "Sure, Finley."

McKeever played for an hour, a dull game with dull people, made so by constant association, by wearing out all avenues of conversation. He listened to the rain on the roof, and to their talk, and managed to stay out of it whenever he could.

SOMEONE came to the front door and pounded on it. Finley Fineen, turned his hand face down and went out to see who it was. He came back with a worried-looking man in a rain-soaked coat.

"Been some trouble," Fineen said and sat down at the table.

McKeever looked at the man. "What's wrong, Ben?"

"An accident, Sheriff." He looked at the others, as though wondering whether he should talk or not.

"Its all right," McKeever said. "Better tell me about it."

"My wife and I were driving into town," the man said. "Got a late start because one of my cows was about to drop and I had trouble—"

"Spare us the details of this bovine delivery," Harris said dryly. "Get on with it, Ben."

"Well, it's Dalridge, Sheriff. He's dead. We found his rig overturned on the road south. I didn't look at him too good, but he sure was dead."

McKeever sighed and got up, putting on his slicker. "I'd better get out there. This is the second Saturday in the month and Dalridge would be carrying a lot of money."

"You think someone around here has light fin-

26

gers?" Stanton asked.

"No," McKeever said, grinning, "but the mine owners will feel better if it's locked up in my office." He touched Ben on the arm. "Thanks for stopping, Ben."

"It was the least I could do," the man said and went out.

"This makes four-handed poker," Harris said. "Damned dull."

"I'm for closing it up," Daley said suddenly, and then looked as though he wished he'd kept quiet.

Harris was putting on his coat and hat. Fineen made an appeal. "Hell, you stay, Doc."

"No," Harris said. "Better get out to Ludlow's place. Shouldn't keep a woman waiting, or so they say." He glanced at Stanton. "Wade, what's your wife going to say if you come home early tonight?"

"We're not speaking," Stanton said flatly. "The first peace I've had for two weeks, believe me."

"I believe you," Harris said and went out with Mc-Keever.

Fineen waited until he heard the front door close, then put the cards away. The shine of sweat appeared on his face and Wade Stanton laughed. "Nerves, Finley?"

"It was tighter than I thought it was going to be," Fineen said. "A lot tighter."

"Let's look at the money," Daley said. "I want to go home."

"In a minute," Fineen said. "We want to make sure we got everything straight. All right?"

"Sure," Stanton said. "There's nothing like a straight story."

"The rain will wash out the tracks," Fineen said. "And that's important. Now there's no use fooling ourselves; we counted on McKeever finding out that Dalridge was robbed. Had everything gone as we'd originally planned, it would have turned out no different than now."

"Only Dalridge is dead," Daley said.

"So he's dead," Stanton said. "Hell, a man of sixty is about through anyway, ain't he?"

"That doesn't matter," Fineen said flatly. "McKeever will know it wasn't an accident when he finds the dead horse. But we're in the clear. Just keep remembering that."

"I'll remember it," Stanton said. "Now let's split the money."

"All right," Fineen said and went to the desk to get it. He took it from the sacks and stacked it neatly, then began to count. Stanton and Daley watched, nervously, until it was placed into three equal piles.

"Nearly eighteen thousand apiece," Fineen said. "That's profit."

"I thought it was going to be twenty," Daley said. Stanton looked at him sharply. "What's the hell's the matter with you, Bill? You getting greedy all of a sudden?"

"Oh, shut up, both of you," Fineen said. "Now I'll leave it up to each of you to hide this right. If it's found by anybody, we're all in it together." He leaned forward. "Now listen to this. We trust each other; there's no other way. As long as we go on trusting each other, we'll come out fine. But I know McKeever, and if anything ever leads him to any of us, he'll start hammering away. We've got to make damn sure that nothing leads him here, understand?"

"Yeah, we understand," Stanton said.

Fineen looked sharply at him. "Wade, don't take this lightly."

"Who the hell's taking it lightly?"

"You are," Fineen said.

"Dalridge is dead," Daley said.

Stanton looked at him. "S'matter, you afraid to use the word murder?"

Daley looked as if he was about to strangle. Fineen's scowl was like a rain cloud forming. "You got a blunt mouth, Wade."

"Yes, I have." Then he smiled. "It doesn't take much to get us arguing, does it?"

"You trying to prove something?" Fineen asked.

"No," Stanton said, "but I'd like to point out a few facts, Finley. Granted that you figured a lot of things right, like the habits Dalridge got into without knowing it, and making the gun out of that hunk of pipe, so it could be put back afterward and no one would ever know what it was used for. And the way we hit Dalridge—all very neat, with the rain to cover us, and our own habits to back 'em up. Hell, I'll bet McKeever would swear on a stack of Bibles that we never left this office, because we've met here every Saturday for years." He shook his head. "That was real good planning, Finley. But you made a couple of mistakes."

"Like what?"

"Like misfiguring the money. You're right so much of the time that I thought you'd be right there too."

"You complaining because you're short a few thousand?"

"No, just pointing out that you could make a mistake. You made another when you killed Dalridge." He held up his hands when Fineen started to speak. "All right, you had to do it; I won't argue that, but it was a mistake."

He got up and began to put on his hat and coat. Fineen watched him carefully. "Don't blow this, Wade. I mean it. Watch that wife of yours."

"Hell, she'd be the last one I'd ever tell."

After he left, Bill Daley slipped into his coat. Fineen said, "Don't let this work on your mind now."

"How can I help it?" Daley asked. He looked along at Fineen. "Finley, what in God's name ever led us to this moment?"

"Does it matter? We're here." He made a motion with his hand. "Go on, get a good night's sleep. I've got some cleaning up to do."

He went out in back after Daley went home, and took a shotgun bore brush to the pipe, scouring it so that all trace of powder was gone. Then he went back into his office and took out the three guns they had used. He recognized the one he had carried; the barrel was matted with blood and hair, and a few other things he didn't want to look at.

A strong drink of whisky helped; then he sat down

to clean the .45. By the time he was ready to reassemble it, he found himself thick-fingered, for he had drunk nearly half the bottle.

"Get ahold of yourself," he said softly. "I mean it, Fineen."

3.

A DOZEN MEN JOINED LINCOLN MCKEEVER AROUND the upset buggy, and a ring of lantern light illuminated the scene. McKeever motioned for Jim Singleton, a young man who ran the hotel and doubled as deputy sheriff. McKeever was examining the horse, and Singleton cast the glow of his lantern over the animal.

"Someone must have used a stick of dynamite," McKeever said softly. He raised his head and looked at those crowded around the buggy. "Keep away from there! Too many tracks already!"

He listened to their muttered resentment and understood the reason for it. Even Jim Singleton said, "Lincoln, to hell with the horse. Hadn't you ought to get Dalridge out of the mud?"

"In a minute," McKeever said. "Jim, see if you can't send that crowd home."

He stood in the rain while Singleton argued in his mild voice. Finally a few men returned to their buggies; others followed once the movement commenced. When Singleton came back, he was alone.

"This damn rain has washed all tracks away,"

McKeever said. "Even the ones Dalridge made when he went off the road." He took the lantern from Singleton's hand and walked over to the dead man, examining him carefully. Jim Singleton looked over McKeever's shoulder, trying hard not to lose his supper.

"Ain't his legs busted, Lincoln?"

"Yes. I guess the wheel caught him when the buggy went over." He held the light closer to Dalridge's head. "He didn't crack his skull in the fall though." McKeever pointed. "There's nothing but mud in that ditch, Jim."

"Yeah." The young man swallowed hard. "This ain't no accident, is it, Mr. McKeever?"

"No, it's murder. And robbery, unless we find that money." He turned to his horse. "I'm going to leave you here until I can send Doc out with the ambulance."

"Gosh," Singleton said, "I ain't even carryin' a gun."

"You won't need a gun," McKeever said, and then turned back. "Here." He took a break-open .32 Smith and Wesson from his inner coat pocket and handed it to Singleton. "This ought to make you feel better. It is damn dark out here, and the rain makes a man jumpy. And I can think of better company than a dead man."

McKeever mounted and paused to look back. Singleton was standing by the edge of the road, lantern in one hand, pistol in the other. McKeever kicked the horse into motion and rode back to Two Pines.

He could tell by the milling, muttering crowd that

the word had gone around, and as he rode down the street, men followed him, pushing questions at him, questions he did not bother to answer. . . .

There was a telegraph in Two Pines, owned jointly by the Idaho Lumber Company and the Galena Mining Company; McKeever dismounted in front of the building and turned in the doorway, facing the men crowding up. "There's nothing you can do," McKeever said. "Why don't you go about your business? Everything's being taken care of."

"You goin' to leave Dalridge out there in the rain?" one man asked.

"Doc Harris knows about it," McKeever said. "He'll go out there with his ambulance as soon as he's able to." McKeever went inside the telegrapher's shack. To the telegrapher, he said, "Did you notify Burgess at the mine, or Kelly at the mill?"

"No, sir," the telegrapher said. "This office only transmits messages; we don't originate 'em, Sheriff."

"You're a good man, Larry. All right, let me have a blank." McKeever wrote for several minutes, then gave the messages to Larry, who tapped them out to a mute length of wire. Immediately he was answered; the camps were only a few miles away, and they kept an operator on duty all the time.

McKeever waited for the answers, read them, then dropped the paper into his pocket. When McKeever turned to the door, the telegrapher said, "Mr. McKeever, someone killed Dalridge for the money, huh?"

"Yes. There's no use in trying to keep it a secret. I'll be at the Hanover House if anyone wants me."

He stepped out into the downpour, but kept under the overhangs as he walked toward the hotel. There was a mild-mannered crowd on the porch, full of unspoken questions, but McKeever passed into the lobby and hung up his dripping coat. The dining room was dark, closed for the night, but McKeever knew there was coffee in the kitchen; he went there, turned up the lamp, and took a cup from the cupboard.

WHILE he drank, light steps drew nearer, and Nan Singleton paused in the doorway. She was tall, like her brother, and fair-haired. Her eyes were large and her lips full. "Where's Jim? Out there all alone?"

"He'll be all right," McKeever said.

"Because you say so?"

"There's nothing out there to harm him. Nan, he's twenty. Let him be a man."

"I suppose there was nothing out there to harm Dalridge either?"

He shrugged. "I won't argue with you."

"Some of the men think it wasn't an accident."

"It wasn't," McKeever said. "The old man was killed for the money he carried."

Nan Singleton seemed horrified. "Lincoln, the murderer might still be out there someplace."

"I doubt it. Likely he's on a fast horse and riding as far as he can go."

"Then why aren't you chasing him?"

McKeever smiled. "After I talk with Burgess and Kelly, I'll telegraph to all the towns within a hundred miles and tell them to look for strangers who have a lot of money to spend, or are in a hurry. The fastest horse alive can't outrun the telegraph."

"That's a lazy man's way of doing a job," Nan said, and went back to the lobby.

McKeever took his time with his coffee and when he was through, he washed the cup and laid it on the drainboard of the sink to dry. The lobby was crowded; every chair was taken, and men stood in small groups talking earnestly. When Lincoln Mc-Keever stepped into the room, they stopped talking and looked at him, their expressions curious, and annoyed, and angry.

Sam Richardson, who ran the bank of Two Pines, as mayor spoke for all of them. "What are you going to do about this, McKeever?"

"Catch the man," McKeever said. He peeled the wrapper from a cigar and put a match to it.

"Then why ain't you out looking?" one man asked.

McKeever raised his eyes and looked at the man. Nan Singleton stood behind the mahogany counter, waiting. "Which direction did he take?" McKeever asked.

Richardson snorted. "How in the hell would Pete know? McKeever, you move too slow to suit me. You always have."

"What do you want me to do?" McKeever asked. "Richardson, when a man asks for a loan you just give it to him, or ask a few questions first?"

"This isn't the same thing," Richardson said. He shook his finger at McKeever. "Dalridge had a lot of friends around Two Pines, friends who'll want to see someone hang for this. He carried a lot of money in his day, and not one penny stuck to his fingers."

The lobby drained by common consent; they all followed Richardson outside. When the door closed, Nan Singleton said, "You're not the most popular man in town right now, Lincoln. I feel a little sorry for you."

"Do you?"

"Yes, you have a large responsibility."

Lincoln McKeever smiled faintly. "That's a refreshing change, Nan. You usually believe that I have too little responsibility." He put on his hat and coat and went outside, discovering that the rain had stopped. Eaves still shed water, and it drained away in the gutters, but the clouds had broken, allowing a moon to shine through.

He walked two blocks over to his office and let himself in. The room contained a damp chill and after lighting the lamp, he built a small fire in the potbellied stove. Settled in his chair, with his cigar, Lincoln McKeever wondered where a man started to unravel a murder.

Of course the money was motive enough. McKeever wasn't certain of the exact amount, but it was always enough to make carrying it risky. Still, old man Dalridge had been carrying money for years, and never lost any of it. There was that time when a lone man tried to hold him up and got both barrels of buckshot in his chest for his trouble. After the county buried the man, no one else ever bothered Dalridge.

And Two Pines wasn't the kind of town where violence spawned. It was dull, but so were a lot of towns back east that had long ago settled into their comfortable rut. McKeever's home town had been like that, so dull that his father couldn't stand it any longer and had pulled out. Things like murder and robbery happened in Tombstone and Dodge City and El Paso, but not in Two Pines.

McKeever's cigar turned into a sour stub and he went to the door to toss it into the street. While he stood there, Doctor Harris drove by with his ambulance. Across the way, Wade Stanton observed this passage from his saddle. Stanton saw McKeever and came over and dismounted. As he stepped inside, Jim Singleton came down the walk, his long step quick and determined.

Singleton closed the door, then laid McKeever's pistol on the desk. "Jim," McKeever said, "when Doc finishes, I want a report."

"What for?" Jim Singleton said. "Hell, you can tell that the knock on the head killed him."

"Tell Doc I want it in writing," McKeever said. "You'd better go on over to the hotel, Jim. Your sister's worried about you."

"Let her worry," Singleton said and slammed the door as he left.

"There's a damned fresh kid," Wade Stanton said. "He's shot his mouth off to me a couple of times. One of these days I'm going to set him down, hard."

"Jim's just crowding his growth," McKeever said. He picked up his gun and broke it open, spilling the cartridges onto the desk top. He got out cloth and oil and dried it thoroughly.

"Why don't you carry a man-sized gun?" Stanton asked.

"What's wrong with this?"

"A thirty-two? Hell, when you go up against a man, you need a bigger gun, that's all." He shook his head. "Dalridge's killing's sure got this town jumpy, you know it?"

"I didn't think they'd take it calmly," McKeever said. He reloaded the Smith & Wesson and slipped it into his pocket. "They'll cool down in a day or two, after they get a chance to think about it."

"Who could have done a thing like that?" Stanton asked.

"Someone who wanted money," McKeever said.

"Maybe some down-and-outer passing through," Stanton said. "That could be worth thinking about, Lincoln."

"Oh, I'm thinking about it," McKeever admitted. "But that poses a lot of unanswered questions. How did he know Dalridge was carrying money?"

Stanton shrugged, then said, "Could be he was hoping to get a few dollars and hit a bonanza."

"Mmmmm," McKeever said. "A possibility there. Then, I have to ask myself who would be carrying a stick of dynamite around just in case he wanted to hold up someone."

Wade Stanton laughed. "I'm going home. Everytime I suggest something, you blow it apart for me." He got up and turned to the door. "Betty's been asking why you never come out any more."

"Wade, don't you know?"

Stanton shrugged. "Hell, Lincoln, there was never any jealousy on my part. I thought that was over with you. Over a long time ago."

"Sure, it's over," McKeever said. "She made her choice and I let it go at that. But it might start talk."

"To hell with the talk," Stanton said. "I enjoy your company, Lincoln. So does Betty. How about tomorrow; it's Sunday. Right after church, huh?"

"All right," McKeever said and watched Stanton leave.

He looked at his watch, and wondered whether or not he should wait for Olin Kelly and George Burgess. Then he decided that they'd be here when he got back, so he slipped into his coat, got a lantern out of the back room, and went to the stable for his horse.

McKEEVER left town, taking the south road, and when he got to the wrecked buggy, he dismounted, tied his horse and put a match to the lantern. His curiosity was jabbing him sharply, and he didn't like it, especially his curiosity about the dead horse.

The dead animal had attracted his attention from the beginning, so much so that he had glossed over his examination of Dalridge. And even now, he could not clear his thinking of the dead animal. Every time he tried to think of a possibility, the horse kept cropping up, as though begging him to come back for a closer look.

Damned funny, McKeever thought, that a holdup man would choose this way to stop a horse and buggy. Shoot the horse, perhaps, or the driver, but to blow up the horse—only a warped mind would think of that.

McKeever spent twenty minutes examining the animal, especially what appeared to be an entrance wound just behind the left shoulder. A very big hole, too big for a rifle. He measured it with his fingers and found it to be nearly an inch and a half in diameter.

He disliked this work, the blood and the torn flesh, yet it was necessary; his curiosity was stronger than his distaste. Quite obviously this was not the work of dynamite; some kind of a projectile was used, and McKeever could not find an exit hole.

The horse's back had been broken from inside, which suggested an explosion to McKeever. This had led his original thinking to dynamite. The intestines were ruptured, and much flesh had been torn away. He did not doubt it now; the animal had been killed by a fired shell.

McKeever stood by the road, thinking about this. A damned big gun was needed to shoot a shell that large. Too big for a man to handle easily, or get rid of in a hurry.

He blew out the lantern and rode back to his office.

Doctor Harris was there, his foul pipe filling the room with shag tobacco. His report was on McKeever's desk. As McKeever hung up his hat and coat, Harris said, "The head injury killed him. I'd say he was struck repeatedly by a gun barrel, or an iron rod."

"How big a gun?"

Harris shrugged. "A handgun. Of course, it could have been an iron rod."

"All right; that's something anyway." McKeever bent over the lamp to get a light for his cigar. "Doc, go get Jim Singleton and a couple more men from the stable. They'll loan you a block and tackle and rope. Get that horse on a wagon and cut him open. Bring me anything you find."

"What? Lincoln, I'm a doctor, not a vet!"

"Will you do this? For me?"

"All right," Doctor Harris said, edging toward the door. "Have you lost your mind? God, the people here'll howl their heads off when they find out you're investigating the death of a horse."

"Let 'em howl," McKeever said. "Did Kelly or Burgess get into town yet?"

"They're at the hotel," Harris said, and stepped out. He paused to look back. "Do you know what you're doing, Lincoln?"

"No," McKeever said. "But don't worry about it."

4.

WADE STANTON'S RANCH LAY IN THE FORK OF TWO valleys, less than an hour's ride from Two Pines; yet he loitered, not wanting to arrive home too early. Betty would want to know why, and Wade Stanton wasn't too sure he could carry off an excuse.

Then there was the money; he'd have to hide that before he went into the house. He wasn't worried about the four paid hands; they had been in Kincaid's saloon and had a four-hour thirst to quench.

The mud made his approach silent and he dismounted by the barn, turning the horse into the stall before unsaddling. With the saddlebag over his arm, Stanton walked around the barn to the corral. With a shovel he dug a hole at the base of the manure pile, then went back to the barn for half a dozen burlap sacks. He wrapped the saddlebag carefully and then covered it, smoothing manure over the spot.

After he put the shovel away, he walked to the house, noticing that the parlor lamp was still lighted. He scraped the mud off his boots, then paused just inside the door to take them off. No need to get Betty started by tracking in mud.

He went into the parlor, and a moment later her bedroom door opened and closed. She came in, eyes pinched to shut out some of the light. "You're early. Lose all your money playing poker?"

"The game broke up," he said. "There was some trouble."

He looked at her briefly. She was small and shapely, dark-haired and quite tan. She was young, in her early twenties, which was an immature age as far as Wade Stanton was concerned. "Why don't you go back to bed?" he asked.

"I'm awake now," she said and sat down. She let the robe fall away from her legs, long enough for him to have his look, then she pulled the folds tightly around her.

Stanton said, "You do that on purpose, don't you?"

"Do what?" She looked at him innocently.

"Never mind," he said. "You'd say I was making it up."

"Well, you make up so many things," Betty Stanton said. . . . "What kind of trouble?"

"What? Oh, Dalridge was killed." He forced his voice to be casual.

"That's terrible! Does Lincoln know who did it?"

Stanton shook his head. "I invited him for dinner tomorrow."

"Why did you do that?"

He shrugged. "I thought you'd like it, that's all."

"You're lying to me, Wade. It's over between Lincoln and me, and you know it. It was over when we got married."

"I suppose," he said. "But it seems a shame. You'd have made a fine pair."

"That was meant to be unkind," Betty said. "But if I had it to do over again, you know which way it would go, don't you?"

"Yes, you've told me often enough," Stanton said. He turned to the sideboard and a glass of whisky. "One thing that's never occurred to you, Betty, is that I'm as sick of you as you are of me."

"Can you really be, Wade? I don't think it's possible."

He sat down across from her, his expression serious. "Betty, where did we go wrong?"

"I really don't know, Wade. You haven't changed a bit, so I guess it must be me. Yes, I think that's it. I wouldn't marry Lincoln because of his job; I thought

43

it was insecure."

"Why don't you be honest and say he didn't make enough money?"

She stared at him for a moment, and then said, "All right, so he didn't make enough. You did. You rode a fine horse and sat a silver-mounted saddle, and I wanted the things your money could buy. But I never got them, Wade. I never got to touch a damned dollar, did I?"

"Betty, you have credit in all the stores. Anything you want to buy is there waiting for you. Hell, I've never denied you anything."

"You've denied me money," she said flatly. "I just want to hold it in my hands, to feel it, to know it's mine. Wade, do you know what I'd do if I could get my hands on some cash?"

"No, what would you do?"

"I'd leave you." His startled expression pleased her. "I'd leave you to your damned Saturday night poker buddies, and your man talk, and your damned man town." She got up then. "Good night, Wade. And don't bother to pound on my door."

When her bedroom door closed and the lock snapped, Wade Stanton poured himself another drink and sat with it in his hands, wondering how a man ever got into such a mess. Take that little tramp he'd known a few years back over in Woodland; she could cook the finest meals a man ever ate, sew on a button in nothing flat, make a man laugh when he felt like slugging the world, and give him one hell of a time in bed. But she was just a nester's daughter, who could

44

hardly write her name, and who'd never dressed decent in her life.

No, Stanton decided, a man had to have better, especially when he had a big place and a bank account, and a responsibility toward the community. So a man chose someone else, Betty Richardson, who some day would inherit a bank. But the old man would sure have to die first because he was too tight-fisted to give away a nickel, even to his own daughter. Maybe that was just as well, Stanton figured. If Richardson ever gave Betty twenty dollars in cash, she'd light out and leave him standing there while everyone laughed.

Wade Stanton was a man who never let a thing bother him until he was ready to let it, and in the silent house, with the lulling effect of the whisky, he thought about Dalridge and the furious, well-planned twenty-one minutes out of his life. Twenty-one minutes that he could never recall or change or wipe out or even forget, for in those minutes a man had died while three other men had taken a step that was final and absolute.

With numbing clarity, Wade Stanton realized that he had known his last restful night on this earth; from that moment on he would have to be on guard for that small mistake every man might sooner or later make.

"Only my mistake will hang me," Stanton said softly, and then went at the rest of the bottle in earnest.

DAL Leggitt reminded Lincoln McKeever of an undertaker, not a newspaperman, for Leggitt was very tall and always wore somber clothes. McKeever opened the hotel room door and found Leggitt there,

45

ink stains on his shirt sleeves, paper and pencil in hand.

"I understand that Mr. Burgess and Mr. Kelly are here, Sheriff. I thought maybe I could get a statement."

"Let him come in," Burgess said. "That all right with you, Kelly?"

"Who can hide this?" Kelly said, and McKeever closed the door.

Kelly and Burgess were both big men, money big, physically big. Forty years of hard work and hard living and a hard heart had elevated them to a position of importance in Two Pines, and wherever lead or timber was sold.

"Have a chair, Mr. Leggitt," McKeever said, and sat down on the edge of the bed. "You were saying, Kelly?"

"I was saying that we ought to post a reward," Kelly snapped. "Dalridge worked for both of us; we split his salary right down the middle. And he was carrying money from both our companies."

"How much money?" Leggitt asked.

Kelly pursed his lips. "I'd say nearly forty-five thousand from me. How about you, George?"

"About that," Burgess said. He made a fuss with his cigar before he put a match to it. "Ninety thousand is a fortune, gentlemen. I hardly need say that I'm more interested in catching Dalridge's killer than I am in recovering the money. A firm in San Francisco has insured all my finances while in transit. I'll file a claim tonight with them."

46

"Then they'll send an investigator?" Leggitt asked.

"I suppose so," Kelly said. "I'm insured by the same firm." His glance touched McKeever. "I wouldn't let any grass grow under my feet if I were you, Lincoln. Hate to think of an outsider poking his nose into our business. I'd like to see this cleared up locally."

"So would I," McKeever said. "And believe me, gentlemen, I'll do my best."

"Just get the killer," George Burgess said. "That'll satisfy everyone."

"Sheriff," Leggitt said, "I'd like a statement from you. Any leads?"

"Nothing definite," McKeever said smoothly. "However, I've sent telegrams to all the law enforcement agencies within a hundred miles in every direction, warning them to be on the lookout for anyone who spends money freely, or acts suspicious. I'll question them as they're picked up."

"Seems to be a long way around the track," Kelly said, then popped the lid on his watch. "I want to get off a telegram tonight. San Francisco won't do a damned thing until Monday morning. Probably won't send a man until Tuesday, or even Wednesday." He pursed his lips. "If he takes the train to Woodland, it'll be Friday before he gets here. That gives you a little less than a week, McKeever. Better get on your horse."

"Yes, it isn't much time." When Burgess and Kelly got up to leave, McKeever said, "Ah, about the burial, gentlemen. Do you want the county to take care of that?"

"County be damned," Kelly snapped. "Dalridge was our employee, and we'll see that he gets the best planting possible. I want this town closed up tighter'n a drum tomorrow. Set the funeral for eleven o'clock and pass the word around that I want everyone to be there."

"Why bury him so soon?" Leggitt wanted to know.

Kelly stared at him. "Why not? He's dead, ain't he? And you give the funeral a nice coverage in the paper, understand. And don't put it on the back page, either."

They went out and after the door closed, Lincoln McKeever said, "Don't take Olin Kelly too literally, Dal."

"Oh? Why don't you let me be the judge?"

"All right," McKeever said. "You do as you please. You will anyway."

Dal Leggitt smiled. "McKeever, we never liked each other, but I'm not going to use this killing as a club."

"Well, thanks."

"You just do your job and I won't complain."

Lincoln McKeever smiled. "Did you ever hear the one about not being able to please all the people all of the time?"

"I know that one," Leggitt said. "But I've never jumped on a man's back without a good reason." He stood up then and put away his writing material. "I'll stay out of your way, Lincoln. I imagine you have things to do."

"I have, for a fact," McKeever said and went down to the lobby with Dal Leggitt.

Nan Singleton stopped McKeever before he could

48

make the sidewalk. "Lincoln, it's after eleven. Where's my brother?"

"With Doc Harris."

"Send him home."

"If Doc's through," McKeever said.

Temper bloomed in Nan Singleton's eyes. "I said send him home." She whirled and went into the back room, slamming the door behind her.

The clerk, who had observed this with a smile, said, "What makes you two fight?"

"Ask her."

"Wouldn't do any good," the clerk said. "You know, I think you're both afraid you'll stop fighting."

McKeever frowned. "What the hell's that supposed to mean?"

"You figure it out," the clerk said, and then laughed.

Doc Harris was operating in the stable, with Jim Singleton handing him instruments and seeing that the lanterns were shining properly. Harris looked up briefly when McKeever came in. A cloth had been spread on a cobbler's bench, and bloody pieces of metal were piled there.

"How's it going?" McKeever asked.

"You want to know something?" Harris asked. "You've got me curious now. This horse is peppered with hunks of metal." He dug for another piece. "I'll be at this all night, the rate I'm going."

"It'll help if you get all the pieces you can," McKeever said.

Doc Harris squinted. "What you going to do, Lincoln? Make a puzzle out of this?"

"It's been floating around in my mind," McKeever admitted. He glanced at Jim Singleton. "Your sister wants you home."

"I'm helping Doc," Jim said. He was a round-faced young man, in spite of his height. "Do I have to go?"

"Not unless you want to," McKeever said.

He watched Harris work, then he heard the town clock strike midnight. A step in the stable archway made him turn, and Nan Singleton stopped there.

"I thought I said that I wanted Jim home."

McKeever walked over to her. "He's busy. We're all busy, so you go on and mind your own business, Nan."

She sucked in her breath and glared at him. "I'm not going to argue with you, Lincoln."

"That's a change," McKeever said. He took her arm and turned her away, but she tried to twist out of his grip. He held her, until she tried to kick him, then he unexpectedly pulled her against him and kissed her. For a second she was passive in his arms; then she writhed away, pawing the back of her hand across her mouth.

"Don't you ever do that to me again!"

"Afraid you'll get to liking it?"

"Lincoln, I hate you!"

"What for? Not because I kissed you. Or is it because I didn't kiss you soon enough?"

"I'm not Betty Stanton," she snapped. Then she looked at her brother. "Jim, you come home, you hear?" When the boy didn't answer, or turn his head,

50

she stamped her foot. "Then stay, damn it! See if I care."

"Nan—" McKeever began.

"Shut up! Just leave me alone." She turned and ran down the street, her skirts lifted above the mud.

Doc Harris turned his head and smiled. "She likes you, Lincoln."

"Oh, to hell with you," McKeever said.

"Don't be stupid as well as blind," Harris said. "She likes you too much, and you hurt her at one tine or another." Then he turned back to his job of probing the horse's carcass for bits of metal.

5.

LINCOLN MCKEEVER HAD HIS HORSE SADDLED before dawn, and when a wan, cloud-filtered sun rose, he was again examining the overturned buggy in which Dalridge had died. The rain had washed out all the tracks, leaving the road a smear of undefinable gouges, and McKeever did not favor them with even a moment's attention. He looked along the road in both directions, looking for a hiding place, a haven for ambush; he was sure that Dalridge had been taken by complete surprise, for no other way would have succeeded.

McKeever thought about this. How did you take an old Indian fighter by surprise? No place for a man to hide, unless he crouched in the ditch, and McKeever scratched that out for two reasons: a man on foot is in a poor position to escape, and then there was the gun—how big he wasn't sure, but certainly bigger than a heavy rifle. With that ruled out, McKeever thought of a horseman and immediately discounted it because of the gun.

Another buggy? That was worth considering; he mounted and rode back a piece until he came to the lane leading to the main road. Stopping there, he could see the wrecked buggy, and the elements began to fall into place, at least enough so that every idea he got wasn't automatically shot full of holes by conflicting evidence. In the first place, Dalridge wouldn't be alarmed by a buggy coming up behind him. McKeever stopped. A buggy would be just right to carry an infernal gun the size necessary to shoot an exploding shell.

Then he took out a cigar and began to gnaw on it. Why an exploding shell? Why not just shoot Dalridge? Hell, he was clubbed to death anyway. McKeever's brows wrinkled as he thought about this. Then an answer came to him. Confusion was what the robbers were after, something to confuse the hell out of anyone trying to make head or tail of this. Killing the horse to stop a man was something new and confusing in highway robbery, McKeever had to admit.

McKeever puffed on his cigar and considered himself to be a robber, bent on robbing but not on killing, and then in the end forced to kill. What would make a man kill? Recognition? McKeever slowly took the cigar from his mouth. By God, how simple could he get? Of course that was it! Dalridge recognized one of the men and was killed because of that.

The facts then piled up in McKeever's mind too fast to sort.

This was no outside robbery; the men who robbed Dalridge lived in Two Pines. Men? The fact that he had thought of them in the plural surprised him, and he groped for the reason his thinking had automatically taken that turn. In a moment he had it—the gun. Too big for one man to handle and drive at the same time. Two men anyway, he decided; one to drive and one to kill the horse.

Mounting his horse, Lincoln McKeever rode slowly back to town, kicking possibilities around in his mind. The more he thought about it, the clearer it became. Almost everyone in town knew that Dalridge carried money from the mine and the logging camp, and the robbers would have to know that in order to set their trap. Know the back roads too, in order to get in and out of town without being seen.

McKeever almost wished that some stranger had killed Dalridge; finding him would be easier than ferreting out someone in Two Pines. He knew everyone, yet he knew none who seemed capable of this robbery and deliberate murder.

"But it's my job to find out," McKeever said softly, and then rode on to his office.

HE shaved and changed into his best suit, and when he was wiping the mud off his boots, Doctor Harris came in, bleary-eyed and in a foul humor.

"I said it would take all night." He set the metal fragments on McKeever's desk. "You have a good sleep?"

"I didn't bother to lay down," McKeever said.

Harris packed his pipe and lit it. "What you going to do with all that scrap junk, Lincoln?"

"Try and put it together," McKeever said.

Doctor Harris shook his head. "Lincoln, you'd better not spend your time fooling around with that thing. Folks would like it a lot better if you started hunting around for Dalridge's killer."

"I intend to get to that too," McKeever said.

"Well," Harris said, "I never knew a man who could tell you what to do. Me, I'm going to shave and get ready for the funeral. When Kelly and Burgess say for a man to be someplace, it pays him to listen."

McKeever grinned. "They don't scare you, Doc. Who're you fooling, anyway?"

"Kelly and Burgess," Harris said and went out.

McKeever unwrapped the cloth and spread it out on his desk, sorting the pieces carefully. Harris had washed them in alcohol to clean them, and McKeever chose the largest fragment as the starter. He sorted and fitted until he found another fragment that seemed to fit properly, then he stopped, wondering how he was going to glue this together.

Finally he got the idea of using putty; he got a half-used can from the storeroom. He scraped the dried stuff off the surface and then molded a piece into a ball, pressing the metal fragments into it. They clung to the putty, and he began to put his puzzle together.

McKeever had fit four pieces together when Dal Leggitt came in. He sat down and said, "McKeever, I want to put the paper to bed this afternoon and I wondered if there was anything you wanted to add to it?"

"Nope," McKeever said. "You may say that this office has no leads. I'm completely in the dark."

Leggitt's brows furrowed. "You want to admit that?"

"Why not?" McKeever asked. "Don't you want to print the truth?"

"With election only six months away, I thought you'd have something better than that." He looked at the scattered fragments of metal. "What the hell are you doing?"

"Trying to find out what killed Dalridge's horse."

"Good God, who cares about the horse?"

McKeever looked at him. "I do, Dal. Don't you?"

"To hell with the horse! What do you think the readers are going to do when they hear you're investigating the death of a horse?"

"Mob me?" McKeever shook his head. "Why don't you go print your paper, Dal? I'd hate to think that the women in this town would be without it to wrap their garbage in."

Color ran into Leggitt's face, and he stood up quickly. "All right, McKeever. I'll give you war, if that's what you want."

"You just do that," McKeever said. "You intended to anyway, in spite of the speech you made for Kelly's benefit." McKeever bored the man with his eyes. "You know something, Dal? If Nan would marry you,

55

you'd get off my back, wouldn't you?"

Leggitt stood there and for a time McKeever thought he wasn't going to answer. Then Leggitt said, "I don't like you, McKeever. I don't like any man who takes what I want."

"I have no claim on Nan Singleton, and you know it."

"You've got the kind of a claim I can't break," Leggitt said. "But I'll break it, Lincoln. I'll break it and you at the same time." He rubbed his thin, ink-stained hands across the front of his coat. "You hurt her, McKeever, and you're going to pay for it."

"Get out of here," McKeever said. "Go on, beat it."

"All right, but remember what I said." He backed to the door, then eased out, as though he were afraid to turn his back on McKeever.

FINLEY Fineen's head felt like a number-two washtub when he awoke, and his mouth seemed stuffed with cotton. He got up, stood for a moment in his underwear, then staggered to the wash basin and soaked his head in the cold water.

Then he realized that he hadn't even gone home; he didn't want to think of what his wife would say. Dressing, he threw away the empty whisky bottle, then went out through the yard in back, took a side street to his house on Locust Street, and tried to ease in the side door without making any noise.

His wife was in the kitchen; she came to the hallway, flour-covered hands on her hips, and the very devil in her eye. "Finley Fineen, where have you been?" Without waiting for an answer she approached him, sniffing suspiciously. "You smell like a mince pie!"

She was a small woman in her middle thirties, and still pretty in a sun-bleached way. Fineen looked downcast. "I got drunk, Madge."

"Finley, you didn't?" She seemed horror-stricken.

He nodded. "I did, Madge."

"You gave me your pledge the day we were married, Finley."

"Aye, and for eleven years I've kept it." He raised his head. "By God, Madge, a man's got a right to go on a toot once in a while!"

"I'll have no drunks in my house," Madge Fineen said. "You know I feel strongly about liquor, Finley." She compressed her lips in that firm way she had. "Now you march right upstairs and take a bath and change your clothes. They're burying that poor Mr. Dalridge this morning and the whole town will be there."

"This morning?" Fineen straightened. "I didn't know."

"Of course you didn't know. How could you, being drunk?"

"Ah, Madge, are you going to harp about that for the next twenty years now? If it isn't one thing, it's another."

"Now, Finley, you're a respectable man, and you've got to set a good example." She made shooing motions. "Go on now. We haven't much time."

He sniffed. "Is that pie I smell?"

Her smile started slowly; she could never long contain anger. "I thought you'd like it, Finley."

He came to her then and put his huge hands on her shoulders. "Madge, you're a woman in a million, do you know that?"

"I don't think I ought to let you touch me," she said, then came against him, her arms around him tightly. "You worried me so, Finley."

"Now, now," he said, kissing her briefly. "You're not really mad at one, are you?"

"Well, since this is the first time in eleven years—"

He laughed then and went on up the stairs, whistling.

Fineen brought his clothes down to the small room off the kitchen, and there filled the wooden tub with water. He sang in an off-key baritone while he scrubbed, then dried himself and slipped into clean underwear. While he was buttoning up, he suddenly stopped singing and jerked open the door leading into the kitchen.

Madge Fineen had her back to him and she was pummeling a piece of bread dough on the table. Finley Fineen locked his hands against the door frame and closed his eyes as her fist beat the dough with a dull sloughing impact. The sound beat against his ears and brought sweat to his forehead and upper lip.

Finally he could stand it no longer. Roughly he shoved her aside, unmindful of her surprised cry. Then he picked up the bread dough and threw it out into the back yard.

"Finley, have you lost your mind!" She tried to take

his arm, to pull him around to face her, but he jerked away.

"Don't ever make that stuff when I'm home, you understand?" He shouted.

"Finley, you lower your voice! You want the neighbors to hear?"

He looked at her, his expression set. "I don't give a damn about the neighbors! Now you mind what I say!"

"What in the world's gotten into you, Finley?" She shook her head and tried to laugh. "I've made bread every Sunday morning for twenty years. My mother made it on Sunday morning, and her mother before that."

"I don't give a hoot what they did," he said. "I'm telling you, Madge, don't ever make that stuff again while I'm in the house."

"Finley, I don't understand you at all," Madge Fineen said. "I just don't understand you at all. I can't see what making bread has to do with you getting so upset."

"Just never mind," Fineen said, calmer now. "Madge, I've never been a demanding man, and you seem happy with me."

"Oh, I am, Finley. You've been all a woman could ask in a man."

"Then just mind me this time, huh? Is it so much to ask?"

"No, but I don't like to break my habits, Finley. No more than you do." Her brow wrinkled slightly. "What would you say if I just asked you to give up something, without telling you why?"

"Madge, you can buy your bread from Hanson's Bakery!"

"I prefer to make my own," she said, then smiled. "Go get your clothes on, Finley. A man looks so funny in his underwear." Then she looked out the door at the bread in the yard. "My, and it would have made such pretty loaves too."

Fineen went into the side room again, closed the door, and, leaned against it a moment. When he felt that his control was restored, he slipped into his suit, then went out so that Madge could knot his tie.

She was in the yard gathering the pad of dough, her expression sad, as though he had destroyed something fine. When she came in, she dumped it into the garbage pail and put the lid on.

Fineen said, "Madge, honey, don't be angry with me, please."

"If drink does this to you, Finley—"

"Yeah, I guess that's it." He licked his lips. "I told Bill Daley I'd drop over this morning. I'd better do that, I guess."

"Land's sake, don't you see enough of him on Saturday night? All right, you'd better go; you'd just faunch around here if you didn't. But you come back here in time to take me to the church."

"Sure," he said, and turned to the door.

"Finley Fineen! You come here and let me fix that tie."

6.

McKEEVER WAS STANDING ON THE PORCH OF THE Hanover House when Finley Fineen turned the far corner. Wade Stanton was coming down the street in his buggy and when he saw McKeever, he pulled over to the hitchrack and stopped. Betty sat beside him, a wide hat shielding her face. She smiled at McKeever and said, "I got up early this morning and baked an apple pie for you. I expect you to appreciate it."

"I'll show that appreciation by eating two pieces," McKeever said. "Going to the funeral?"

"Of course," Stanton said quickly. "I liked Dalridge too, you know."

Fineen crossed the street, nodded to McKeever, then said, "Don't you think that striped shirt is a little gay for a funeral, Wade?"

"That's what I told him," Betty said, "but he never listens to me."

"Funerals are too sad anyway," Stanton said. "They can stand a little cheering." He glanced at Betty. "And don't start crying; you didn't know Dalridge that well."

"One is expected to cry a little," Betty said.

"A barbaric custom," Stanton said. "I'll bet half the women have onions in their handkerchiefs."

McKeever seemed offended. "You have a practical mind, Wade. Too damned practical."

"Well," Fineen said, "I'll see you at the funeral, huh, Wade?"

"Why, sure."

Fineen nodded to Betty and walked on.

Bill Daley lived over the drugstore, and Fineen went up the outside stairs. Daley's wife answered the door, a pleasant-faced woman with the sharpest tongue in town, a startling contrast to her gentle appearance.

"Oh, it's you," she said. "Come on in."

"Is Bill up?"

"Yes, but he hadn't ought to be," she said. "I told him to stay home last night, but he had to play poker. This wet weather raises hob with his health, but poker's more important." She snorted. "Seems to me he's trying to make a widow of me before my time. Deliberate, if you ask me."

"I'd never make the mistake of asking," Fineen said.

She glared at him, hard eyes in a sweet face. "He's in the parlor. Go in if you want to."

Bill Daley heard them talking and came to the hallway. He had a towel around his throat and a thermometer in his mouth. He spoke around this. "I'm not long for this world, Finley. Didn't sleep a wink last night."

"You coming to the funeral?"

"I'd better not," Daley said. "This cold's worse. Real bad."

"You'd better come," Fineen said. He glanced into the kitchen to see if Daley's wife listened. "You want this to look good, don't you?"

"Hell, it'll look all right if I'm not there," Daley said

softly. "Everyone knows how sickly I am."

Fineen tapped him on the chest with his finger. "Bill, you show up at the church and at the cemetery, you understand?"

"Oh, all right." He had a fit of coughing. "I ought to go to a dry climate, Finley. Arizona or someplace where the air's good."

"To hell with that," Finley Fineen said. "Once you got clear of Two Pines you'd start spending that money."

"I wouldn't," Daley said. "Honest, I wouldn't, Finley."

"Where would you get the money to live on then? You think your wife would give it to you?" Fineen laughed softly. "She's got you buffaloed, Bill. I'll bet she prays you'll come down with something and die, leaving it all to her."

"Ah, you got no right to talk like that," Daley said. He shook his head. "Must have got wet last night. I've got no resistance for these things. Doc Harris said so." He took Fineen by the sleeve. "Look, if Doc advised me to go to another climate, who'd suspect, huh?"

"We'll talk about it later," Fineen said. "Now get dressed for the funeral."

He went to the door and let himself out. Daley's wife waited until Fineen's step faded, then came into the parlor. "I don't think much of your friends."

Daley looked at her. "That's not surprising, Ethel." He went into the bedroom and laid out his dark suit.

"You're going to the funeral after all?"

"Yes," he said.

"Fineen talk you into it?"

He turned to her, exasperated. "No. Fineen didn't talk me into it. I feel better, that's all."

"My, what a miraculous change. A few minutes ago you felt too bad to answer the door. Made me come all the way in from the kitchen to open it."

"Ethel, don't make it sound like a twenty-mile hike."

"You're sharp to criticize, aren't you?"

He bit his tongue and slipped into his pants and shirt. "I wouldn't criticize you, Ethel. Some people are just born perfect, and you're fortunate that you're one of those rare jewels."

"That's right, throw it up to me. Always throwing it up to me. What do you have to go to the funeral for? What was Dalridge to you?"

Daley hesitated, then said, "I don't want to go, Ethel; I wish I didn't have to go. But I'm a business man and it would look bad if I didn't." Then he shrugged. "Besides, birth and death are events that happen only once to a man. What's in between doesn't matter very much."

He knotted his tie, picked up his hat and coat and went to the door, his wife trailing him.

"I suppose you'll stop off for an afternoon with your crowd. I won't see you until suppertime."

He paused in the doorway. "Will that break your heart, Ethel?"

She looked at him a moment, then her lower lip began to quiver and tears dammed up against her lower lids. "It just breaks my heart to see us this way, Bill. I don't mean to be talking all the time, picking at you, but I just can't help myself. Sometimes I think you'd be happier if I was dead."

This talk alarmed him, although he had heard it before and recognized it for an attention-getting device. He put his arm around her and patted her on the shoulder. "Don't think about things like that, Ethel. We get on as good as most."

He left her at the top of the landing and went on down to the street, coughing into his handkerchief.

THE minister preached a fine sermon, a little on the solemn side, but fine, the kind every man wanted spoken over him, glossing over his bad points and stretching his good ones as far as credulity would allow. McKeever sat through it, his attention wandering, and after the church emptied, the minister came up to him, speaking in that soft, confidential voice he had so patiently cultivated. "Sheriff, I haven't had time to select the pallbearers. Kelly volunteered, and Burgess, but I wondered if I could count on you?"

"Certainly," McKeever said. He looked around and saw Finley Fineen talking to Wade Stanton and Bill Daley. "I'll get the other three for you." He walked over and they broke off their talk. "Goodnight wants some pallbearers. I've elected you three."

"Hell," Stanton said quickly, "I don't want to carry a casket."

Fineen fixed him with a sharp eye. "What kind of

talk is that, Wade? Sure, Lincoln, we'll serve. Be proud to."

"I don't think I ought to lift anything," Daley said. "Feeling the way I do."

"A sixth of two hundred and fifty pounds isn't much," Fineen said. "You can count us in, Lincoln."

"Thanks," McKeever said and walked away.

Wade Stanton glanced around him to make sure no one was near enough to overhear. "My God, Finley, where's your feelings?"

"Hidden," Fineen said. "And that's where yours ought to be." He looked at Daley. "Wipe that sick look off your face, you hear?"

"Finley, I—I don't want to carry him."

"By God you're going to carry him," Fineen said softly. "This isn't what I want, but if it has to be, then we'll do it." He discovered sweat on his face and wiped it away. "I got drunk last night." He was instantly sorry that he made the admission, for both Daley and Stanton looked sharply at him.

"I didn't sleep a wink," Daley admitted. He glanced at Stanton. "How about you?"

"I never thought about it," he said quickly. Then he chuckled. "I think both of you have paper guts."

Fineen tapped him on the arm as Lincoln McKeever came over. "Goodnight's ready. Wade, you want to pick me up at the office after the funeral?"

"Sure," Stanton said. He took Bill Daley by the arm. "Come on, let's get Dalridge in the ground respectful-like."

McKeever was not fond of funerals, and the crying,

but he endured it, and as soon as possible he walked back to his office. He barely had time to light a cigar when Olin Kelly and George Burgess walked in and sat down.

They looked sad-eyed and silent, as though their dearest friend had just passed away, and this annoyed McKeever and goaded him into speaking. "You can quit acting now."

Both men looked at him, offended. Kelly said, "What a hell of a thing to say. Dalridge was our employee."

"He was a man who worked for you and now you'll hire another one." McKeever leaned on his desk. "Have you notified the insurance company?"

"Yes," Burgess said. "I expect a telegram tomorrow. I'll let you know if they're sending a man or not."

"It won't make much difference if they do or don't. I think our man is still in town." He put it out for its shock value, and found that it had plenty.

Both men tried to talk at once, but McKeever quieted them and told them why he thought the killer was still in Two Pines.

"By God, McKeever," Kelly said, "this is horrible. I thought we had honest folks around here?" He turned his head toward the door as Stanton drove up in his buggy. Kelly and Burgess put on their hats. "We'll see you later, Sheriff," Kelly said. "Come on, George. I want to think about this for a while."

"Make sure you don't talk," McKeever said. "And I mean to anyone."

"Don't worry about that," Burgess said, and they

67

went out, meeting Wade Stanton as he came in the door. McKeever put on his hat while Stanton took a look at the clay and metal fragments on McKeever's desk.

"What you making, mud pies?"

"Just something to pass the time," McKeever said. When Stanton went to pick up the clay, McKeever said, "Don't do that, Wade. I don't want it disturbed."

"Hell, I was only looking," Stanton said, frowning.

He walked to the door with McKeever, then stood there while McKeever locked up. Betty was waiting in the buggy, her hat in her lap.

"I'll get my horse," McKeever said.

"Ah, Lincoln, I want to stay in town for a while. Why don't you drive Betty home and I'll ride your horse out when I come?"

McKeever frowned. "Wade, I can wait if you won't be long."

"I don't know how long I will be," Stanton said. "Hell, I trust you, Lincoln."

Color came into McKeever's cheeks and he glanced at Betty Stanton, but she was studying her fingernails. Without looking up, she said, "Am I going to have to waste the pie?"

"All right," McKeever said and climbed into the rig. He lifted the reins and drove out of town.

FINALLY Betty Stanton said, "Don't look so glum, Lincoln. There are men who would like to be alone with me."

"Men you were once engaged to?"

"That was two years ago," she said. "I thought it was all over."

"It is, but people still like to talk."

She laughed. "Lincoln, a little talk would liven up this dead town."

"It's lively enough to suit me," he said.

She made a half pout with her lips. "Now you're talking like Wade. All he wants to do is eat, sleep, and raise hell with the boys."

"You're complaining?"

"I get lonesome," she said. "Don't you?" She took his arm and tugged. "Stop this damn thing for a minute."

He hauled on the reins and then she turned in the seat and put her arms around him. Her lips came against his, warm and working, speaking to him without words. Then she drew away, laughing, her hands smoothing her hair. "You know, I needed that, Lincoln."

"Now you've made me sorry I came with you," McKeever said.

"Why? Are you afraid Nan Singleton will find out?"

"What do you have against Nan? You've been digging at her for two years."

Betty Stanton shrugged. "Lincoln, I made a mistake, marrying Wade."

"So?"

"So I'd like to straighten that out."

"What's that got to do with Nan?"

"Well, she's in love with you, Lincoln, and I don't want her to be." She touched his cheek gently, then

69

kissed him again, lightly. "I want to get away from Wade. And when I do, I'm going to make right the mistake I made two years ago. I want you, Lincoln. And I want you unattached. To get you that way I have to say just the right things to Nan Singleton. Not lies, really, but I want her to think the worst. And Lincoln, I don't think you really mind. Do you?"

He blew out a long breath and sat with the reins lax in his hands. "Betty, I wish I could get over you."

"You never will," she said. "Now come on, let's go home. Wade may stay in town for hours yet."

7.

WADE STANTON WALKED TO FINLEY FINEEN'S office, hoping to find him there, but Fineen was home, with his wife. Stanton stood by the door for several minutes, trying to decide whether to go to Fineen's house or send for him. He decided that sending for him was safer, so he collared a boy and gave him two twenty-five-cent pieces, one for fetching Fineen and the other for fetching Bill Daley.

For ten minutes Stanton waited, and he forced himself to appear unconcerned. It wouldn't do to seem nervous; someone might see him and remember it; for the town was full of people who liked to look in on everyone else's business.

Bill Daley arrived first, a trace of annoyance in his expression.

"What the hell is this?" Daley asked. "I had a devil

of a time explaining to my wife. You know I'm not good at thinking up excuses."

"Do you have to tell your wife everything?" Stanton asked. Then he saw Fineen coming down the street.

Fineen frowned and said. "There's no reason for this, Wade. What excuse are you going to offer for this?"

"I'll tell you inside," Stanton said.

"Not to me, you fool," Fineen said. "What are you going to say when someone starts prying into your reason for coming here today?"

"Nobody will," Stanton said.

"The hell they won't. Before the day's out you're going to be asked. How about it? What's the excuse?"

"Oh, tell 'em that Bill ordered a new buggy for his wife."

Daley looked surprised. "Buggy? I haven't given Ethel a gift for ten-twelve years."

"Then it's time you did," Fineen said and unlocked the door. He said no more until they were in his back office, with the door closed. "All right, Wade, what's up?"

"I just came from McKeever's office. You know what he's doing? He's putting together the pieces of that shell."

"So?" Fineen said.

"So he'll find out about it!" Stanton snapped.

"By God, I made that shell," Daley said, alarmed. "Finley, what are we going to do?"

"We're going to do nothing," Fineen said. He looked at each of them. "What the devil do you expect me to

71

do? Steal it from him?"

"Why not?" Stanton asked. "Finley, McKeever's at my place, with Betty. He'll stay there until I get home, so we've got the time."

Finley Fineen frowned. "What's this? About McKeever being with your wife, I mean?"

Wade Stanton waved his hands. "It don't have anything to do with us, Finley. But we can take advantage of it."

"Everything the three of us do and say has to do with all of us, and don't you ever forget it, Wade." Fineen's frown was intense. "What are you cooking up for McKeever's benefit anyway?"

Wade Stanton hesitated, then said, "Well, Betty and I don't get along; I'd be better off without her. But she's expensive, Finley. I'd have to kick her out without a cent, but I need a reason to do that."

Fineen blew out his breath. "So you want to involve her with Lincoln McKeever, is that it?"

Shrugging, Stanton said, "Well, hell, they were pretty sweet on each other once, so I thought—"

"You're bragging!" Fineen snapped. "No one ever accused you of thinking, Wade. Now you listen to me, both of you. Don't cook up any schemes of your own, understand? We made a plan and we're going to stick to it. So McKeever's putting together the pieces. All right, what does he have when he gets through?"

"Something I made," Daley said. "And I don't want it traced to me."

"He can't trace it to you," Fineen said quickly. "You made that shell in my shop, in the hours when you were supposed to be playing poker, in the hour before McKeever came here each Saturday night. Now, I mean it, we don't get panic-stricken over this."

"I still think stealing it—"

FINEEN cut Stanton off. "That would be the worst thing we could do, Wade. Then and there McKeever would know that the men he wanted were right here in Two Pines." He shook his head. "We leave him alone, you understand. I'll go see Dal Leggitt at the paper; he's always had it in for McKeever. If I drop the hint that McKeever's wasting his time putting pieces of metal together, Leggitt will blast him with his paper."

"But if he can rebuild the shell," Daley said, "he might find the gun."

"What gun? There isn't any gun," Fineen said. "That was part of the idea, using parts of this and that to fire the shell. A gun is something that has to be gotten rid of, but not our gun. There's nothing for him to find. Hell, he could use my press for the rest of his life and never suspect that he was handling the gun barrel." He took each of them by the arm, steering them toward the door. "I tell you not to worry about this. I'll see Leggitt and get him stirred up, and you two just stand back and watch the fireworks; we'll keep McKeever on the fire until he's tired of jumping around."

"All right," Daley said, "but I still think—"

"What can we do?" Fineen asked. "What can we possibly do that won't throw suspicion our way? We must make sure that McKeever never knows for sure that the men he wants are still in Two Pines." He patted their shoulders. "Now get out of here, and Bill, tell your wife in a roundabout way about the new buggy."

"Lord, that's expensive."

"You can afford it," Fineen said. "In fact, you can't afford not to buy it." His glance touched Stanton. "And you came here to see it. After all, everyone knows we're close friends." Fineen smiled. "Relax, Bill. When that mouthy woman of yours gets through telling it all over town, no one would ever think of questioning us about this meeting."

"You're too damned careful," Wade Stanton said.

"Careful?" Fineen shook his head. "I know how people like to talk, that's all. Now go on, get out of here."

AFTER they left, Fineen sat down at his desk and tried to straighten the facts out in his mind. Somehow he could no longer say which was important, to lead McKeever astray, or to sit back and rest in the knowledge that McKeever could never trace the killing to his door.

He was disturbed, now that McKeever was piecing together the shell; Fineen hadn't figured on his doing that at all. To his way of thinking, McKeever was just a man coasting along in a soft job, not particularly smart, and certainly without any experience when it came to catching criminals. The way Fineen had it figured, McKeever would tear up the countryside looking for Dalridge's killer, but he had fooled everyone by staying around town and apparently doing nothing.

Only McKeever wasn't idle; Fineen knew that now. Neither idle nor stupid, and the fact that he lacked experience didn't seem to slow him much.

He believed he knew a way to throw Lincoln Mc-Keever off the track, although it violated his original plan. But after thinking about it, he decided it would be foolproof, and he didn't have to tell Wade Stanton or Bill Daley; what they didn't know wouldn't hurt them.

Removing the money in broad daylight, even with all the doors locked, wasn't the smartest thing Finley Fineen ever did, but he figured that it was necessary. He took eight thousand dollars and set it aside, then put the rest of the money back in its hiding place. Carefully he stripped the band from one package, but made certain that a portion of it, with the mine's name, was placed between the layers of bills as though it had accidentally been caught there and overlooked.

With brown butcher paper he wrapped the money securely, then penciled a note:

Mr. Lon Beasley
Attorney at Law
Woodland, Wyoming

Dear Mr. Beasley:
Here you'll find eight thousand dollars to buy me a ranch with. I hear you buy property and sell it and I've been looking for a place, now that I have the money. You just hang onto it for me and I'll be

75

in a week come Saturday to get the deed. I'll identify myself to you.

Yours,
Peter Hotchkiss

Fineen read it over a few times and seemed satisfied, both with the wording and his disguised handwriting. He tied the bundle and tucked it into his coat pocket, feeling, as he let himself out, that this would draw Lincoln McKeever away from Two Pines like a good dog on coon scent. Fineen was sure that most of the newspapers would carry a story of the robbery, so every sheriff would be aware of what that binding ribbon meant, as would Lon Beasley.

Getting the package mailed presented a problem to Finley Fineen, but he solved it by cutting through the Wells Fargo stage yard on his way home. This was not an uncommon route for him and he would arouse no suspicion, particularly when he stopped and looked at the coaches.

The mail was carried in the well beneath the driver's feet, and Fineen knew that the rocking now and then broke open the bags, at least often enough so that the drivers always looked for scattered pieces. Sidling around the coach, Fineen saw that no one was watching through their front windows. He quickly tossed the package into the footwell, knowing that when it was found in Woodland, the driver would assume that it had been spilled out of the sack.

No one would be able to trace the package to Finley Fineen.

Walking the rest of the way home, Fineen was troubled, for McKeever had driven him to doing something he swore he would never do: depart from the original plan. From the beginning he had figured that most men got caught because they panicked, and sooner or later, broke cover to run. This was one mistake he was not going to make, and yet he had already made it by allowing McKeever to jar him.

As he approached the house he remembered that he had to see Dal Leggitt, and turned about, walking back up town. Fineen knew better than to go to the newspaper office; this was Sunday and Leggitt would be trying to make time with Nan Singleton.

Leggitt was on the porch of the Hanover House, Nan beside him in one of the wicker chairs. Fineen made his approach casual, and his halt one of those spur-of-the-moment things. Taking off his hat, Fineen inspected the band for sweat stains. Then he said, "Pretty good funeral, huh, Dal?"

"As good as you'll ever see in Two Pines," Leggitt admitted. "The best thing that can happen to a man around here is to die with Olin Kelly's and George Burgess' blessing. Everyone attends then."

Fineen laughed because he was supposed to, then looked at Nan Singleton. "You're a mighty pretty thing today, Nan."

"Thank you, Finley. It's nice of you to say it."

"How many times has Dal proposed this month?" Fineen asked.

"Now cut that," Leggitt said, somewhat quickly.

"Damn it, doesn't a man have any business of his own around this town? Seems to me that there ought to be something else to talk about besides each other." He shook his head as though this were a sad state of affairs. "By golly, I can walk into Huddlemyer's place to buy me a new derby, and the whole town knows about it before I can put it on."

"Yeah," Fineen said, "it's a fact all right. But we're all guilty, Dal. We all talk too much." He squinted a look up and down the street. "I guess you heard about McKeever's new project."

"What project?" Leggitt asked.

"You mean you haven't heard?"

"Get to the point, Finley!"

Fineen grinned. "I couldn't believe it when Wade told me. Betty invited Lincoln out for dinner, but Wade stayed in town." He paused, leaning forward to lower his voice. "I guess it's sort of a secret, but Bill Daley's getting a new buggy for his wife. A surprise. I—ah, had a picture of it in a catalog and Wade wanted to see it."

"Will you quit beating around the bush?" Leggitt demanded.

Finley Fineen acted like a man whose best story is being ruined by impatience. "I'm getting there. Let me tell it my way. Well, when Wade went over to McKeever's office to tell him to go ahead with Betty, he saw this thing McKeever was working on. A hunk of clay with little pieces of metal sticking to it. Now ain't that a funny think for a man to amuse himself with when a murder's been done?"

"By golly, it sure is," Leggitt snapped. "I'm going to talk to McKeever about this and he'd better have a good explanation ready."

"Well, you'd better let someone else find out for you," Finley Fineen said. "McKeever and you are sort of out of sorts."

"He'll be more than just out of sorts when he reads the paper," Dal Leggitt said. He glanced at Nan Singleton. "I told you he wouldn't stay away from her."

"Please, Dal." She spoke softly, and did not look at him.

"Did I say something wrong?" Fineen asked, the soul of innocence.

"No, I'm glad you said it," Leggitt said. "Nan, listen to me. I never wanted to hurt you, and I still don't, but you've got to realize that McKeever's not an honorable man. What man would see another man's wife when the husband is away?"

"That's pretty strong," Fineen said. "I'm a friend of both McKeever and Wade Stanton, and talk like that will start trouble." He scratched his head. "It's no secret that McKeever threw Nan here over for Betty, then got pushed out by Wade, but there's been no trouble over it. And I wouldn't want to see none start now."

"There is a thing called honor and decency," Leggitt said. "Would you excuse us, Finley? I want to talk to Nan alone."

"All right," Fineen said. "I'll see you around, Dal."

He turned and walked back to his home, and after he passed out of earshot, Dal Leggitt took Nan Singleton's hand. "Isn't this enough to convince you, Nan? I mean, all she has to do is to whistle and he runs."

"Yes," she said. "I'm sorry I've been so foolish, Dal. Very sorry."

"Nan, Nan, I've waited a long time to hear you say that. Perhaps now you'll think more—kindly of me."

"Kindly?" She smiled and squeezed his hand. "You're good and gentle. I'll marry you, Dal. Whenever you say."

He came closer to shouting then than he ever had in his life, but he was a man nearly incapable of expressing his emotion, never elation such as he knew then. He merely smiled with his eyes and his lips, and said, "This is May. We'll have a June wedding. Tradition, you know."

"Yes," she said softly. "We wouldn't want to start off by defying tradition, would we?"

8.

As soon as Wade Stanton got Lincoln McKeever's horse from the stable and rode out of town, Bill Daley let his worry come out in the open, for this was what he did best—worry. If it wasn't about his health, it was about his wife, but now he had something else to grow concerned about, the scattered bits of the projectile that McKeever was patiently reassembling.

Making the explosive hadn't been at all difficult,

since he had training in chemistry; the projectile itself was an eight-gauge brass shotgun shell with a metal detonator. Still, Bill Daley had fashioned it with his own hands, and because of this, he felt that it could lead the law directly to his door. He wanted to believe Fineen, but he still knew he would sleep better if he had those metal particles in his own possession to destroy.

Getting into the sheriff's office on a Sunday afternoon presented more of a problem than he had first imagined; too many people sat on their porches and saw everything that went on within blocks of the place. Still, fear of one thing can drive a man past another fear, and Bill Daley walked slowly, boldly, down the street, tipping his hat now and then, speaking occasionally to those who spoke to him.

McKeever's door was unlocked and Daley went in, his eyes going immediately to the desk where the scattered pieces lay. The thought that he should just jam the whole thing into his pocket and run was uppermost in his mind, but caution took hold of him, and held him from that bit of foolishness. Too many people had seen him come in; he now wished that he'd gone home instead. If he took it, McKeever would have no trouble at all finding out who the thief was, and Daley didn't want that finger pointed at him.

Instead he took only a handful of the pieces, enough of them so that McKeever would never be able to assemble the thing to the point where he could positively say how it was made, and what it was made of. Daley turned to the door, ready and eager to leave, but stopped when he heard steps coming toward him. Quickly he began to whistle in a sub-tonal key and examine the reward dodgers on the wall.

When the door opened, he turned his head, feigning pleasant surprise. "Hello, Doc. McKeever's out."

"I can see that," Harris said dryly. He squinted at Daley. "What did you do, break the law?"

"Why, no. What made you think that?"

"Just a joke," Harris said and crammed tobacco into his pipe. He sidled over to McKeever's desk and looked at the clay and metal. "Wish to hell he'd hurry up and get that thing finished. I'd like to see what I worked all night to get."

"What's that?" Daley said, turning.

"This—thing," Harris said. "It killed Dalridge's horse."

"No fooling? But who the hell cares about the horse? What's McKeever doing about Dalridge?"

"You'd have to ask him," Harris said. He disturbed the pieces with his finger. "Funny, but I thought I dug out more chunks than that. Anyway it seemed like I did."

"What did you do? Count 'em?"

"I didn't get finished until daybreak," Harris said, stepping to the door. "When McKeever comes in, tell him I want to see him."

"Might as well leave myself," Daley said. "I'll walk with you, Doc."

"All right," Harris said, "but I'm too tired to be much company."

When they approached the hotel, Harris stopped to

talk to Nan Singleton and her brother. Bill Daley smiled and went on toward his place. Harris looked at Jim and said, "You get out of the doghouse yet?" He winked. "If it gets too tough, come over and bunk with me."

"You're a bad influence," Nan said. "Between you and Lincoln McKeever—"

"—we'll make a man out of him," Harris finished for her. "It isn't Jim you're worried about, it's Mc-Keever."

"Doctor, you ought to mind your own business."

Harris laughed. "Why? No one else does in Two Pines. By the way, where is McKeever? Haven't seen him since the funeral."

"He's out to Stanton's place."

"Stanton's?" Harris frowned. "Hell, I saw Wade less than fifteen minutes ago—" He stopped talking and pursed his lips. "Oh, I see what's eating you."

"You don't see anything," Nan snapped. "It's all over between Lincoln and me. I'm going to marry Dal Leggitt in June."

Harris' expression did not change; he sucked on his dry pipe and then put it into his pocket. "Good luck then. You'll need it."

When he walked on down the street, Jim Singleton said, "You sure judge Lincoln fast, Nan."

"Do I? I don't think so. I've had two years, Jim. And two years is a very long time." She got up and started to go inside. "Now don't go running off; there's work for you to do."

• • •

Doc Harris was surprised to find Bill Daley waiting for him. Harris hung up his hat and tossed his bag onto a low table. Daley said, "I guess you think it's funny, me coming here like this, but I haven't been feeling too well, Doc." He sniffed to prove it.

"You've got a store full of pills," Harris said, "and you've tried them all. What do you expect me to do, Bill?"

"I don't know," Daley said. "Maybe I ought to go to Arizona for the dry air."

"Then go."

"Well, I wanted a doctor's advice first."

"I just gave it to you," Harris said. "Pack up and go."

Bill Daley moved his hands briefly. "I don't know what Ethel will say."

Harris blew out a long breath. "Bill, that's your problem. Why bother me with it? I'm dog-tired." He shed his coat and then rolled his sleeves to wash his hands and face.

"I sure wish you'd examine me," Daley said. "A man likes to know what ails him."

Harris raised his head and looked at him, water dripping from his face. "You want to know?"

"Sure."

"You want it straight? All right. The only thing that's bothering you is yourself. Get out of this damned dead town and go somewhere. Get yourself a woman, one of those wide-hipped wild ones who'll take your money then run off with another man. And when that

84

happens, get drunk and stay that way until you land in jail. When you sober up enough to know who you are, you'll be a well man."

"What would I tell Ethel?"

"Tell her? Hell, hit her on the head with something—" Then he shook his head. "No, don't do that. Don't do anything. Just go on listening to her yapping at you all the time and go on selling pills and licorice sticks and coughing when there's nothing to cough." He yanked a towel off the wall rack and dried his face. "This is a tough world, Bill, but be glad you're alive to enjoy it. A man dies too damned quick as it is. I was thinking of Dalridge, working steady, saving his money—and what did it get him but a smashed head."

"That sure isn't pleasant to think about," Bill Daley said.

"No, it's not," Harris said. "Now I'm a tough man when it comes to seeing people die, but I'll tell you, Dalridge's killing got me here." He thumped himself on the heart. "It's one thing to crack a man over the head when you're mad at him, but it's another to keep clubbing to make sure he's dead."

Daley looked at Harris with a set expression. "Is that the way it happened?"

"Yes, it is," Harris said. "You know, a doctor can tell a lot from a wound. I've just figured it all out, what was used, and what kind of a man did it."

"Is that a fact?"

"Yep. He used the barrel of a forty-five and he was a big man, six foot and at least a hundred and eighty-five pounds. I could tell by the damage; a man would have to be that powerful to crack a man's head that bad. Literally pulped the bone."

"I—wish you wouldn't talk about it," Daley said.

"Huh? Oh, sure." Harris chuckled. "I get a little clinical at times." He reached for his coat. "But I guess McKeever will be glad to hear it though."

"Yes," Daley said. "I guess he will." He got up and as he did, he brushed his coat against the back of the chair; the metal in his pocket grated with the musical sound that brass always possesses.

Harris frowned. "You got a pocket full of nails, Bill?"

"Just some junk," Daley said. "Well, I'll see you later, Doc."

Harris opened his door leading onto the outer office. "You ought to take my advice."

"I might," Daley said and offered to shake hands.

The offer was unusual and Harris hesitated, then gripped Daley's hand, glancing at it at the same time. Daley struck him then, the blow catching Harris alongside the jaw. He reeled back, stunned, coming against a glass-faced cabinet full of instruments. The cabinet went over with a crash and Daley drove into him, hitting him again. When Harris fell to the floor, Daley bent and picked up a scalpel, slashing with it before Harris could duck.

He opened Harris' face to the bone, then struck him in the throat, trying to reach the jugular vein. Daley wanted to make this quick, but that wasn't the way it was to be; Harris fought like a wild man and Daley plunged the knife again and again until Harris lay still.

Slowly Daley got to his feet and threw the scalpel away from him. His sleeves were soaked with blood and he quickly shed his coat and shirt. Going to Harris' closet, he put on a clean shirt, then one of Harris' coats, a brown one like the one Daley discarded.

He wrapped his own clothes in a newspaper, then let himself out through the back door where the alley was protected by a long, high wooden fence. At the end of the alley he had a quick look in both directions, then stepped boldly to the walk. At the next block he crossed over and entered the alley behind his own place, and let himself into the back of the store. He could hear his wife walking around upstairs, and quickly rolled up a newspaper to start a fire in the furnace.

The coat and shirt were burning well before he realized that the metal pieces were still in the pocket. Then he decided that it didn't really matter; they would be melted in the fire, destroyed beyond hope of recovery.

ETHEL Daley came to the top of the landing and yelled down at him. "Bill, is that you?"

"Who did you think it was?" He wished she'd fall over the railing and break her neck.

"What in the world are you doing?"

"Building a fire," he said. "What does it sound like?"

"In May? Daley, I've got the windows open."

"Well, I'm chilly," he said. "Go in and quit hollering."

"Don't give me any of your sass!" she snapped and slammed the door.

When coat and shirt were completely burned, Daley went to the wash stand and carefully scrubbed his hands. Reaction was beginning to maul him now and the enormity of his act came home to him.

I made a mistake; this was his thought, and he felt a need to talk to Fineen, only he dared not. Fineen had told him to leave this alone, and he had meant to, only Fineen would never believe that. He hadn't meant to kill Harris. Or maybe he had at that, especially after Harris caught him in McKeever's office.

Bill Daley knew Harris; the man never let go of an idea once his mind locked on it, and Harris would think some more about those pieces of metal, the ones that were missing. And Harris would add them to Bill Daley, more especially after they jangled in Daley's pocket. I had to kill him; Daley rationalized to himself. But it was bad, very bad. Worse than Fineen breaking Dalridge's skull with that .45 barrel. Then Daley remembered Harris' talk. No need to worry about that now; no need to tell Finley Fineen a thing.

But Fineen would know. As soon as someone discovered Doc Harris' body, Fineen would add two and two and come up with the right answer. Bill Daley didn't like to consider Fineen's anger when he did.

He went upstairs then, but left Harris' coat behind.

I'll have to get rid of that, he thought; Ethel will know it isn't mine.

She was in the kitchen and glared at him as he stepped into the hall. "I swear, Bill Daley, sometimes I believe you've lost your mind."

"Don't start nagging, Ethel. I don't feel well."

"Have you ever felt well? I ask you, have you ever felt well? Since the day we've been married it's been complaints day in, day out."

"I think I'll go to Arizona," Daley said. "I was talking to Doc Harris and he said I could clear up this cough in the dry air."

"Go. See if I care."

"But I need money, Ethel. Maybe a thousand dollars. You've got that much saved."

"I'm saving that money," she snapped.

He looked at her for a moment, then a hardness came into his voice. "By God, Ethel, don't fool around with me! Don't drive me now! Just don't!"

She put down her spoon and came up to him, her expression puzzled. "Bill, what's come over you? Your expression, your voice—why you sounded ready to kill me."

"Don't tempt me, Ethel." He whirled away from her, afraid again that he had gone too far, revealed too much.

9.

LINCOLN MCKEEVER DID NOT LIKE WALKING, AND the two-mile hike back to Two Pines was no exception. The walk was of his own choosing but the distance was an accident, brought about by his stopping the buggy, handing the reins to Betty Stanton, then dismounting and saying a brief good-by.

She was an angry woman, and he was a fool, he told himself as he walked back to town. Hell, even a dog will catch a bone if it's thrown at him. But I'm not a dog, McKeever decided.

The walk left him sweating and muddy so he went directly to the Hanover House for a bath and a change of clothes. When he came down the stairs, he found Nan Singleton behind the counter, trying to make the books balance.

"Lincoln, is seven times nine fifty-six or sixty-three?"

"Sixty-three," he said. He looked out through the front window. "The town's like a tomb."

"This is Sunday," Nan said. Then she looked at him quickly, a hardness in her eyes. "You didn't stay long."

"I never got there," he said.

For a moment she just stared, then said, "What?"

"I said I never got there." He smiled. "And I walked back." She closed the ledger with a snap and started to turn away, but McKeever took her arm, holding her. "Betty's a liar."

"About what?"

"About the things she likes to brag about."

Color came into Nan's cheeks. "Lincoln, there must be some truth there."

"No truth," he said flatly. "But you believe what you want to."

"Lincoln, I want to believe—" Then she shook her head. "But it's hard sometimes." She bit her lip briefly, then added, "I told Dal Leggitt I'd marry him, Lincoln."

For a moment he thought he had heard incorrectly; this stunned him more than he believed it would. "I— wish you the best, Nan."

"Do you? Lincoln, let's be honest this one time."

"All right," he said. "I hope Leggitt drops dead before the sun sets."

Then he wheeled out of the lobby and went out to the porch where a cooling breeze fanned him. Jim Singleton had his feet cocked to the railing he shot a glance at McKeever, then toed the chair around.

"You going to bite somebody, Lincoln?"

McKeever laughed; he felt he had to, or explode. "Not today," he said and stripped the wrapper from a cigar. "How'd you like to be a paid deputy, Jim?"

"You mean it?"

"Yes," McKeever said. "I can use you, Jim, and you might as well get paid for it."

"Wow! Can I carry a gun?"

"I expect you ought to," McKeever said softly. He

looked across the street as Dal Leggitt came from his small newspaper office; he had a paper under his arm and headed directly toward McKeever.

"Nan tell you about her and Dal?" Jim said.

"Yes," McKeever said.

Leggitt came up with his prancing step and plopped the newspaper in Lincoln McKeever's lap. "Read that and laugh, if you can," Leggitt said.

McKeever calmly unfolded the paper and read the headlines.

"Sheriff incompetent, eh?" He rolled the cigar from one corner of his mouth to the other. "Violation of public trust? Your punctuation is excellent, Dal, and I believe your spelling is picking up."

Jim Singleton sniggered, then choked it off.

"Irresponsible and lax in his duties—" McKeever looked up. "Dal, don't you think lazy would have been a better word? Right here—" He turned and pointed to the printing. "You've got to choose your adjectives more carefully. Now shiftless is a good word if you want your writing to have impact." He folded the paper carefully, then quickly reached up and slapped Dal Leggitt across the face with it before throwing it into the gutter.

Leggitt raised his hand to his stung cheek, then said, "McKeever, you shouldn't have done that." He shed his coat, popped his cuff links and then carefully rolled his sleeves.

Jim Singleton, with all the foolishness of youth, raced off the porch and down the street, yelling, "Lincoln McKeever's going to whip the hell out of Dal Leggitt!"

Had he sounded the fire bell he wouldn't have attracted more attention. Leggitt stepped forward and cocked his fists. "I'm ready whenever you are, Lincoln."

"You've been ready a long time," McKeever said, and hit him.

Leggitt went into the porch rail, and over it, arms flailing for balance, legs dancing. Nan Singleton came out in time to see this brief flight to the boardwalk.

"Lincoln, how could you hit a man unaware?"

Without glancing at her, he said, "When a man takes off his coat and rolls up his sleeves, he's hardly unaware."

Leggitt was getting up, coming up the steps, and a crowd was gathering. McKeever's sweeping arm pushed Nan back out of the way, and left himself open to Dal Leggitt's charge. McKeever was carried against the wall, lip bleeding from Leggitt's blow; his head buzzing, he managed to wiggle free and block Leggitt's jabbing fists.

Somewhere along the line, Dal Leggitt had taken more than a few boxing lessons from a man who just wasn't shooting his mouth off when he claimed to be a fighter. Leggitt had the footwork and the strength to sting McKeever, keep him back where the kicking jabs were most effective.

McKeever's mouth and nose were bleeding and he hadn't got in any more than that first lick. A new caution took hold of him and he realized that he could easily lose this fight if he didn't watch himself more carefully. Leggitt wasn't the kind of a fighter you could walk into, place your toe against his, and swing until the weakest man fell. Leggitt's skill and ability more than made up for his weaknesses, and McKeever started backing up, making Leggitt come to him, making Leggitt carry the fight.

The crowd was thick and interested and shouted a continual encouragement with a divided sentiment. Jim had his sister backed into the doorway where she would be out of the way, leaving the porch to the two fighters.

McKeever had a cut over his left eye, and a nose that felt like a wet sponge. Try as he would, he could not seem to mark Leggitt at all; every time he swung, the man wasn't there.

And every time Leggitt ducked, he found an opening and laced McKeever again, usually drawing blood. Jim Singleton, whose loyalty was with Mc-Keever, had a hard time saving his face, for there was not a man there who doubted now how this was going to turn out.

McKeever was winded and Leggitt seemed quite fresh. He shifted about in that crazy dance of his, feet whispering lightly on the flooring, fists reaching out and connecting with a sound like a slap.

Unable to take much more of this, McKeever stepped in; he had to finish it now or never. He caught another one on the mouth and shook it off, but he couldn't shake off the one under the heart. A clamp came down on his lungs and his mouth flopped open for an instant and he stood there, looking at Dal Leggitt with completely blank eyes before he began to fall.

Someone generously threw a bucket of rain water in his face and McKeever found that he could breathe again, although painfully. He looked around for Leggitt and failed to find him. Then he heard Nan's voice in some faraway place, pleading with Leggitt. An upstairs window banged open and someone in the crowd yelled as clothes began to rain down, and boots, an old rifle, satchels, a small trunk; everything Lincoln McKeever owned cascaded into the street.

Then Dal Leggitt came down, calmly refastened his pearl cuff links, put on his coat and snapped the lapels flat, and spoke to McKeever in a calm, flat voice. "I've just thrown you out of this establishment, McKeever. Find a place to live somewhere else. If I see you here again I'll take a buggy whip to you."

He brusquely pushed his way through the crowd and stalked back to his newspaper office.

THE crowd began to thin rapidly; every fight had to be talked over afterward and none of them wanted to do it in front of the loser. Jim Singleton helped McKeever to his feet, and there was a sharp disappointment in the young man's expression.

McKeever said, "One thing you learn, Jim, is that you can't win them all."

"I thought you was better than him," Jim said hotly.

"Is that the measure of a man, his ability to fight?"

"Jim," Nan said, "go on inside. Go on, now. I'll take

care of this." She waited until young Singleton went on in, then she said, "I didn't want this to happen, Lincoln, but now that it has, I have no regrets."

"I didn't expect you would have," McKeever said. He stanched the flow of blood from his nose, then said, "Do you suppose I could wash up?"

"Of course. Do you want Jim to pick up your things?"

"Yes," McKeever said. "Tell him to take them over to the jail. I'll stay there."

Nan was turning to the door; she stopped and turned back. "Are you afraid of Dal?"

"No," McKeever said.

"You don't have to move out of here," she said. "Dal Leggitt isn't running this hotel."

"Yes, he is," McKeever said. "I just never realized it."

He went into the kitchen, took off his coat and shirt, then washed carefully. His face was badly bruised and his nose was as spongy as an old potato, much too tender to fool with other than a gentle washing.

Nan Singleton stood by the sink, her arms crossed, watching him closely. "What was the fight about, Lincoln?"

"I like to think that my half of it was inspired by Dal Leggitt's newspaper article."

"I didn't ask you what you'd like to think," she said. "Lincoln, somewhere along the line we've lost the knack of talking to each other."

"Maybe we've said all the things there are to be said. Or perhaps we've said too many of the wrong things. Things we can't forget."

"You're right. I wanted Dal to hurt you, Lincoln. Do you understand that? I wanted him to pay you back for the times I stayed awake with the hurt you gave me."

"And it was all pretty needless," he said, dressing again. "The way it turned out, I mean." Then he shrugged. "But we never know how a thing is going to turn out, do we?"

"No. I suppose that's what makes life so interesting."

"Or so full of pain."

He went out then and found Jim carting his belongings to the jail in a wheelbarrow. McKeever looked up and down the street once, then followed the young man, picking up a shirt, one slipper, and a small box that had dribbled off the load.

The storeroom was suitable for quarters and McKeever spent the rest of the afternoon moving in a cot and making the place livable. Jim Singleton didn't stay, and he failed to mention the swearing-in as a deputy. McKeever supposed now that the young man had lost interest; young men considered a job in the light of reflected glory first and remuneration second, and McKeever had recently lost his luster in Jim Singleton's eyes.

WHEN darkness came, McKeever lighted the lamps in the outer office and began to work on his puzzle. He fitted pieces for several hours before he became aware that many were missing. He could not be sure of this, but he seemed to find the pile thinner, the puzzle twice as difficult.

His head ached and his stomach was still upset; he discounted the bruises on his face, and the stiffness. At eight, Olin Kelly and George Burgess came in, their expressions serious; they took chairs and came right to the point.

Kelly did the talking. "McKeever, we heard about the fight you had with Leggitt, and we know the reason behind it."

"Oh?"

"You're taking this calmly enough," Burgess said. "Olin and I read Leggitt's account of your activities; perhaps you could explain them to us. We want to be fair about this."

"What is there to explain?" McKeever asked. "I believe it's important to piece together these pieces and Leggitt believes it's more important to chase all over the country after men who do not exist there. What can be more simple?"

"You're twisting this, McKeever," Kelly said. "George and I have talked this over with several responsible people, and we feel that your affair with Leggitt was more personal than a matter of law-enforcement policy."

"I can't help what you think," McKeever said.

"Let me tell it," Burgess said. "You're getting nowhere, Olin. McKeever, since this crime occurred, you've sent a few telegrams to outlying peace officers, then set on your butt as though you were investigating a hog theft. Now we told you once before that we wanted action. We meant it. And if you can't give it to us, then we'll put someone in office who will."

"I see," McKeever said. "Maybe you gentlemen would like to run this yourselves?"

"Now don't get huffy," Kelly said. "We didn't say that at all. McKeever, did you go out to Stanton's place this afternoon?"

"It's none of your business if I did," McKeever said.

Kelly and Burgess looked at each other. "I thought you'd take that attitude," Burgess said. "McKeever, in view of the fact that you're doing next to nothing about Dalridge's killing, we think it would be best for all concerned if you stepped down."

"Resign? What if I say no?"

"Then we'll put you out of office," Kelly said. "McKeever, there are enough moral people in Two Pines to back us, but we'd rather not drag up anything that would be embarrassing, you understand. Betty Stanton is Sam Richardson's daughter, and we don't want to embarrass innocent people." He paused a moment. "Make up your mind, McKeever. Do you go out the nice, easy way, or the hard way?"

"Will you answer one question?"

"If we can," Kelly said.

"Who suggested this?"

The two men looked at each other. "Dal Leggitt. Who did you think?"

McKeever nodded, then said, "All right, you'll have my resignation in the morning."

10.

BETWEEN THE HOURS OF NINE AND ELEVEN MONDAY morning, Dal Leggitt's paper appeared on the street and was promptly read by every serious-minded citizen in Two Pines. Not that there was ever anything in the paper that the citizens didn't know about, or hadn't talked over already, but it was nice to see it in print. Made it permanent, sort of.

Leggitt was a little put out because he didn't have time to set up a piece on the front page about Lincoln McKeever being asked to resign, but he talked it up, making certain that everyone in town knew about it. At his own expense, Leggitt telegraphed San Francisco and learned the name of the investigator they were going to send; he had a word profile of the man, Charles Boomhauer, on the front page. Leggitt enjoyed giving a story the personal slant; his paper was a small-minded, opinionated rag but the people of Two Pines excused this, feeling that it was better to have a biased paper than none at all. According to Leggitt, the investigator was a whiz who always got his man, and the town of Two Pines would soon see a lawman of genuine caliber in action; this dig at Lincoln McKeever did not pass unnoticed.

Bill Daley caused a mild stir in town by taking delivery of a new buggy, the first new rig he had ever bought, as far as anyone could remember. He parked it in front of his drugstore so that everyone could admire the brass fittings, the red wheels and the shiny black body. Daley stood proudly by while the crowd gathered and he was disturbed to find that the buggy was not the drawing card; people were curious as to why he had abandoned his tight spending habits, and Daley found this hard to explain. He thought he would just say that he bought it for his wife, but everyone knew that they fought, that she wore the pants and that Daley wouldn't give her the time of day. The purchase of the buggy became as big a mystery in Two Pines as the robbery-murder of Dalridge.

Just before noon, one of the men at the mine dropped a setting maul while shoring staging and put a slight dent in Swan Jaccobbson's head, and it was only when they sent a man to fetch Doctor Harris that anyone discovered he had been killed.

Lincoln McKeever was having a mid-morning breakfast at a small restaurant on Ash Street—he'd felt too creaky to get up earlier—and his attention was pulled to the commotion on the street. But he did not leave his table to see what was going on, for Jim Singleton came charging through the door, more than eager to relate the news.

"Somethin' terrible's happened," Jim said.

"What? Leggitt's newspaper office burn down?"

"I'm not joking. Doc Harris is dead."

Lincoln McKeever put his fork down. He saw that Jim Singleton was serious and reached for his hat. They went out together and Jim told him how Harris was discovered as they hurried to Harris' office.

A jam-packed crowd fronted the place and Mc-

Keever rammed a way through for both of them. Dal Leggitt was inside, snooping around, and he frowned when McKeever stepped into the room.

"What are you doing here? This isn't your business any longer."

McKeever did not bother to answer him. He pushed him aside and looked at Harris, who was stiff and blood-caked. It didn't take much of a brain to figure out how Harris had died, but when and by whose hand was some problem.

Jim Singleton looked pale, but more controlled than when he had looked at Dalridge. "Let's go," McKeever said.

As they stepped to the door, Olin Kelly and George Burgess came in. "A terrible thing," Burgess was saying. "Who'd want to kill Doc Harris, the best friend this town ever had." He glanced at McKeever. "You see him? What do you make of it?"

"I could give you only an unofficial opinion," McKeever said and tried to press through.

Kelly stopped him half angrily. "Man, this is no time to get proud."

"Ask the new sheriff," McKeever said.

Burgess frowned. "You know we haven't appointed a man yet. Hell, there's no need to be sore about this, Lincoln."

"Who's sore? Coming Jim?"

They skirted the crowd and stopped on the main stem. Jim Singleton said, "Lincoln, you suppose Doc found out something? About Dalridge, I mean?"

"He wasn't killed for fun," McKeever said. "Well,

there's nothing to be done while that crowd's littering up the place. I'll go back later when they quiet down."

Jim Singleton shifted his feet. "Lincoln, you've resigned. You're not forgetting that, are you?"

"No, but I knew Harris pretty well. He liked to write things down. Some men are like that, Jim; they'd rather write a report than tell something." McKeever looked down the street and saw Finley Fineen come out of his office and stand on the walk's edge. The street was deserted except for these three men, and as McKeever turned to walk toward Fineen, he noticed a fourth, Bill Daley.

HE stopped by Daley, merely because he was nearer than Fineen. Daley said, "Your face looks like hell, Lincoln. Better let me give you something for it."

"Maybe later. You been over to Doc's house?"

Bill Daley shook his head. "I don't have the stomach for it. Besides, a dozen people will insist on telling me about it."

"In this town you'd better make that two dozen," McKeever said and walked on. Jim Singleton decided to go back to the hotel; McKeever sided Fineen and prepared a cigar for a match. "Messy business, huh, Finley?"

"Yeah." Fineen looked at Bill Daley for a long moment, not dropping his glance until Daley went back into his store. "Who could have done a thing like that, do you suppose?"

"A badly frightened man," McKeever said softly.

"You know anyone who's frightened, Finley?"

"Not that scared," Fineen said. "Hey, you suppose Doc's death had anything to do with Dalridge's being killed?"

"I'd say so," McKeever agreed. "But the question is, what was the link? What tied the two together and made killing Doc necessary?"

"Gives a man the creeps, don't it? I mean, a man could wake up dead damned easy."

"Only if he knew too much about the wrong things," McKeever said.

"I guess that's right. If it gets any tougher around here I think I'll move south to Tombstone and do something safe, like drawing on Wyatt Earp." He laughed at his own joke, then choked it off since McKeever didn't think it was funny. "You see Daley's new buggy?"

"I never paid any attention to it," McKeever said. He shifted away from the wall, ready to leave.

"Where you staying now?" Finley Fineen asked.

"A rooming house on Pine. Poker this coming Saturday night? I can come an hour earlier now."

"I don't know," Fineen said. "We'll see, Lincoln."

"What do you mean, we'll see? We've been playing Saturday night poker for years."

"Well, I guess we'll have a game," Fineen said and watched Lincoln McKeever walk away.

As soon as McKeever passed on down the street, Bill Daley returned to his doorway. Fineen cupped his hands around his mouth and called over to him. "A quilted lap robe and a buggy whip goes with that rig, Bill. Come over and get 'em."

Daley hesitated, then said, "There's no one to mind the store."

"Hell, everyone's over to Doc's house." He waited, and finally Daley crossed the street, his expression filled with apprehension and alarm. "Come on inside," Fineen said and closed the door. He speared Daley with his eyes and spoke softly. "I don't have to look far to find the man who killed Harris, do I?"

"I—I didn't mean to kill him," Daley said quickly, softly. "Finley, you've got to believe me."

"Well, I guess no one saw you coming or going," Fineen said with surprising mildness. He smiled and clapped Daley on the shoulder. "You let something stampede you; don't do it again. McKeever's out and there's nothing to worry about. Did you cover your tracks? I mean, you didn't leave anything behind, did you?"

"No," Daley said. "Finley, I'm glad you're not sore. I thought you would be."

"It's all right, I tell you. Look, Bill, we'll just keep this to ourselves. What Wade Stanton doesn't know won't hurt him, huh?"

"Yeah," Daley said, vastly relieved. "It wasn't easy, Finley. God, it sure wasn't easy."

"You'd best forget about it," Fineen said. "Wade will surely suspect that you did it, but that'll be as far as it goes." He smiled briefly. "We're in the clear now. Nothing to worry about. If Doc knew anything, he sure as hell will never tell it. And McKeever's still in the dark. Sure, he might have been getting a lead, but that was all. Now you go on back to the store and keep everything normal, you understand?"

"Sure," Daley said. "How about the robe?"

"That was just something to get you over here in case someone overheard."

"Then let me carry a robe back in case someone looks," Daley said.

Finley Fineen lost his humor. "You tight bastard, you'd milk your mother." He went into the back and brought out a robe, throwing it on the counter. "Take it and get out."

Daley smiled and walked out. Fineen went to the door to stand and when Olin Kelley and George Burgess came toward him, he stepped aside so they could enter.

"Don't tell me I can sell you some more wagons?" Fineen asked.

"No, we're going to try to sell you on something," Kelly said. "All right to sit down?"

"Sure," Fineen said, pushing out chairs. "What's on your mind?"

"I'll come right to the point," Kelly said. "This town needs a law officer. We'd like to have you fill McKeever's shoes."

Finley Fineen had an excellent poker face, and he was smart enough to say just the right things, and exhibit an embarrassed reluctance. "Gentlemen, if it came to hitting a man on the jaw and dragging him off to the lock-up, I guess I could do it, but to investi-gate—"

"We've thought that all out," Burgess said. "Finley, there's a crack investigator coming here from San Francisco, and he'll take over the case completely. But we want a good local man on the job, one that we can trust. Now Olin and I have known you for years. A family man, churchgoer and a responsible business man who's pretty well fixed for money. How about it, Finley?"

He shook his head and frowned; his stalling was misinterpreted for modesty. But beneath it all Fineen was more pleased than he had ever been; they were making everything so, simple for him. "Can I think about it?" he asked.

"We'd like an answer now," Kelly said. "Hate like hell to push you this way, Finley, but we talked it over with Leggitt and Richardson and they're for it a hundred per cent."

"Well," Fineen said, smiling, "I can't buck the local dignitaries can I?"

"Wonderful," Burgess said and offered his hand. "It won't take long to swear you in, Finley." He stuck his thumbs into the armholes of his vest. "The star will look good on you. Takes a big man to represent the law. I guess that's McKeever's main trouble; he just never did look like a sheriff ought to."

"I wonder what my wife'll say?" Fineen said.

"She'll be pleased," Kelly said. "Come on, Finley. We'll get the formalities over with."

Sam Richardson, as mayor of Two Pines, officiated, and afterward he pinned McKeever's star onto Finley Fineen's coat front. There was handshaking all around, and a sample of Richardson's bourbon, which he reserved for state occasions, weddings and funerals. As soon as was possible, Finley Fineen left Richardson's bank, walked a half a block to the hardware store, and there bought a cartridge belt and holster, and a pearl-handled .45 to fit it. With this buckled on the outside of his coat, he stepped to the sidewalk and the admiring citizens.

To his surprise, small boys followed him, for a lawman is youth's highest throne of worship. At the doorway of Daley's drugstore, Fineen shooed them on their way, then went inside. The place was empty of customers and Daley was behind the counter, filling bottles.

He spoke with only half a glance. "Something I can do—" Then he stopped, his eyes fastened on that star. "This a joke, Finley?"

"No," Fineen said. "I was appointed not five minutes ago to take McKeever's place."

"But—but why you?"

"Why not me?" Fineen asked. "I'm a respectable citizen."

Daley looked around, even cocked his head toward the ceiling to determine where his wife was by her footsteps. When he spoke, it was little more than a whisper. "But, Finley, it don't seem right after—"

"It couldn't be more right," Fineen said flatly. "This is a windfall I hadn't counted on, not in a million years. Bill, no one ever suspects a respectable man; I told you and Wade that from the first. Now that I'm sheriff, even temporarily, I'll investigate Harris' killing my own way."

"Finley, I thought you said we'd forget it!"

"Forget it? How can I forget it now? I've got a responsibility to the citizens, haven't I?" He leaned forward. "But don't you worry about it, Bill. I'll confiscate all of Doc's papers and go through them, just in case there's anything there. You know how Doc was, always writing everything down."

"Sure," Daley said, moving his hands nervously. A coughing spell seized him and he fought it under control. "Only this kind of puts us on opposite sides."

"That's all in your head," Fineen said. "You know nothing's changed."

"Hell, everything's changed," Daley said. "God, I only went into this thing because I wanted to see if I could do something by myself. You don't know what it's like to be a little man, Finley. Your wife yaps at you all the time, and kids talk smart to you. Hell, I've never even been in a fight in my whole life."

"Look, don't get stewed up. You know it wrecks your health." He patted Daley on the arm. "You just think about how this is going to be now, Bill. You just think about it and see if it's not better."

Bill Daley shook his head. "I don't know, Finley. I wish to God we'd never started this thing. I don't want the damned money. I don't want any of it, but now I've got it all."

Finley Fineen studied Daley carefully, then said, "There's no out, Bill. If you ever thought there was, you were fooling yourself."

"I know it, and that's what I was doing. Three days ago you and Wade were the best friends I ever had. I mean that, Finley. As long as we just talked about it, it wasn't so bad. But now I don't want to talk to you, Finley, or to Wade. I don't want to even see you any more. You figure that out?"

"Yes," Fineen said softly. "But it's all right, Bill. I'm your friend, you just remember that. One of these days it won't matter."

"What do you mean?" Daley asked.

Finley Fineen shook his head. "It'll work out all right. You'll see that I'm right."

Then he turned and walked out.

11.

WADE STANTON PICKETED HIS HORSE WITHIN visual distance of his ranch, then hunkered down to wait until nightfall. He could see the buggy parked by the porch and this was enough to satisfy him that Lincoln McKeever was still there. Stanton didn't like to wait, but if the prize was big enough, he could do it. He watched the lights go on in the bunkhouse and when he judged that the hands were bedded down for the night, he stepped into the saddle and rode on home.

Easing into the barn, he put up the horse without disturbing anyone, then walked to the house with an eager step. There was a light burning brightly in the parlor, but he expected that. Going around to the back door, he eased it open and catfooted his way down the hall to Betty's room. For a time he stood with his ear to the panel; then he tried the knob, feeling it give in his hand.

With a rush he flung the door open, letting the hall light rush into the room with him. Betty sat up in bed and then laughed.

"What did you expect to find, Wade?" She swung her legs to the floor and turned up the lamp on the night stand. Slipping into her robe, she pushed past him, going into the kitchen.

He followed her, his expression bewildered. "Where's Lincoln McKeever?"

"I wouldn't know," Betty said.

"What do you mean? He came home with you, didn't he?"

"No," she said and stirred the fire. After she placed the coffee pot on the stove, she turned to him. "I've had a bad afternoon, Wade. Very bad. But I've figured it all out now and it's funny. Real funny."

"I don't think it's so damned funny."

"Don't you?" She laughed without humor. "Wade, I wanted to make love to Lincoln, but he got out of the buggy and chose to walk back to town. Can you imagine that, a man walking home? I thought women were supposed to do that. You and I have both been fools, Wade. I want to get rid of you and you want to get rid of me. I wanted Lincoln to take me away and you wanted me to run away with Lincoln."

"Well, as long as it's out in the open, why don't you go?"

"Because he won't have me." She made a wry face. "Honorable men! You can have 'em." The coffee began to boil and she pulled it to one side of the stove. "You looked funny, Wade, sneaking in like a thief, expecting to catch a sinning wife red-handed."

"That's all right," Stanton said. "I can afford to make a fool of myself. You can't."

"I suppose," Betty said. "But I can afford to wait, Wade. Can you?"

"Sure. I'll tell you one thing, though, Betty; you'll never get a nickle of my money."

She smiled and poured herself a cup of coffee. "Want to bet?" She sat down at the table and looked up at him. "This is the kind of a game we're playing between ourselves, Wade, and it'll be interesting to see who wins. You want to make everything my fault, to be the injured party. That way you can slam the door in my face and leave me with nothing. And I want it the other way around. I want to sit in this parlor and own it all, only I don't want you around. Fair enough?"

"That day'll never come," Wade Stanton said flatly.

"Oh, I think it will, if we both work at it," Betty said, then smiled with her eyes as she lifted the coffee cup.

To most people's way of thinking, Finley Fineen was the kind of law officer Two Pines had always wanted, a man on the go all the time. He turned his business over to his foreman, and began a fevered investigation. He went to Judge Harper and got an order to confiscate all of Doctor Harris' papers and belongings, then spent the next two days asking endless questions, especially of the people who lived near Harris. Did they see anything? Hear anything?

Dal Leggitt followed Fineen like a well-trained dog, taking it all down for his paper.

Lincoln McKeever spent his daylight hours in the saloon, playing endless games of solitaire and drinking beer, and to many people in Two Pines this substantiated their earlier belief that McKeever was at heart a lazy loafer.

Now and then Jim Singleton came in with a word about this or that. He disliked the idea of McKeever sitting around doing nothing, and he resented Finley Fineen. This amused McKeever, and he asked, "Fineen turn you down, Jim?"

"Huh? Turn me down for what?"

"You asked him for a job as deputy, didn't you?"

"How did you know that?"

McKeever shrugged. "It just figured. What did Fineen say?"

Jim Singleton frowned, then said, "He told me to get the hell out before he kicked me out. Lincoln, he had no call to talk like that."

"No? You'd better just stay away from him, Jim."

"I will," Jim Singleton said. "Hey, he was asking me what happened to that thing you was working on. You know, that piece of putty and the metal parts."

"It's safe," McKeever said.

"You'd better hand it over before he asks for it."

"If he wants it bad enough," McKeever said, "I'll let him ask." He leaned forward and spoke more softly.

"Jim, one reason I've always liked you is that you can keep your mouth shut."

"Yes, sir. I don't say anything I'm not supposed to."

"I know that," McKeever said. "And that's why I'll tell you this. Let's try to put this thing together using the pieces of knowledge we have. We'll have to assume a lot, but that's all right as long as there's no contradictory evidence. You go along with that?"

"Sure."

"In the first place, we'll assume that the robbers and Dalridge's killers are someone from Two Pines. All right? Second, the only thing we have to work on is the pieces of metal which made up the shell that killed the horse. Now get this clear, Jim: we have no other suspicion; none at all."

"You can say that again. They sure didn't leave anything behind."

"That's fine, but people leave behind more than they figure. A man can leave nothing physical behind, yet leave himself open to suspicion. Those pieces of metal were the one actual link we had with the killer. But what was there about them to make a man afraid? Some of them are missing, Jim. I'd say about half, because I haven't counted the ones that are left."

"Then how can you know that half are gone?"

McKeever smiled. "Doc Harris' report. 'Removed from carcass of dead horse, forty-one assorted pieces of unidentified brass.' That's how I know that half are gone. Look, Jim, you're fresh on this. Let's see what you can make out of this. Harris' killing, I mean. Give me a reason for anyone to kill him."

"Gosh, I don't know, Lincoln. I really don't. Unless Harris knew something that was damaging to someone in town."

"But what could he know?" McKeever asked. "Come on, Jim, think! I want to see if you reach the same conclusion I've already reached. Remember the bits of brass now. Try and take it from there."

"Well, we're supposing that your having them made someone nervous, huh? All right, then is it so far-fetched to suppose someone would try and steal them?" He snapped his fingers. "Sure, someone did steal 'em!" Then his elation faded. "Well, they only stole half of 'em."

McKeever was smiling. "All right, why, Jim? Why just steal half?"

"Hell, I don't know, Lincoln."

"Jim, suppose a man was fixing his watch and he had the parts scattered all over the table and you wanted to play a joke on him, mix him up. What would you do?"

Jim Singleton sniggered. "I'd put in an extra screw." He laughed, conjuring up a mental picture of a man holding a completed, operating watch in his hand and wondering where that extra screw went.

"Suppose you didn't have a screw?"

"I guess I'd swipe some of the parts so he couldn't put it tog—" Then he slapped his forehead. "Sure! Why swipe 'em all when just a few would do the trick?"

"Now you're thinking," McKeever said. "All right,

supposition one is that our man swiped some of the pieces, but where does Doc Harris come in? What have the pieces to do with his killing, anyway?"

"Well," Jim said, "Doc could have come into your office while the man was there."

"No reason to kill for that," McKeever said. "No, Jim, I don't think that's enough. Our man killed out of desperation, out of panic."

"How in the hell can you figure that, Lincoln?"

"Because the job was messy. Jim, if you had a real hate for a man, how would you get rid of him? A man you were really scared of?"

"I'd probably shoot him."

"Well, yes, but you'd do a more deliberate job of it than someone did on Doc Harris. Harris' killer was panic-stricken. He made a horrible mess of Doc's killing. One of those messes a man makes when he's scared to death. You saw the stab wounds, how scattered they were, and you saw Dalridge, and how one spot had been beaten to mush."

Jim Singleton swallowed hard. "I sure don't like to think about it, Lincoln. My stomach ain't none too good around things like that." He shook his head slowly, coming back to the main issue. "Maybe Doc noticed some of the pieces missing? Of course he'd have to say something or the killer wouldn't get jumpy."

McKEEVER reached for his beer glass and leaned back in his chair, a smile widening his lips. "Jim, you've got a head on you. I reached that very same conclusion; no other seems to fit. Of course we're guessing all the way."

"A guess won't hold up in court," Jim Singleton said.

"Sure, but let's see if we can't crowd our man a little. He was scared once. Let's see if we can't scare him again."

"Yeah, but who do you scare?"

"I don't know," McKeever said. "But I'll work on it."

"Maybe Finley Fineen's working on it too."

"Maybe," McKeever said. Then his glance went past Jim Singleton's shoulder to the door. "Here comes Fineen. We can ask him."

Fineen came over to McKeever's table and sat down. He shifted his pearl-handled gun around to the front of his thigh and then leaned his elbows on the table. "Ain't it about time you got a job, Lincoln?"

"I thought I'd live off the fat of the land a little," McKeever said. "You don't object to that, do you, Finley?"

"I got where I am by hard work," Fineen said. "As your friend, Lincoln, I can only say that if you'd applied that rule to yourself you'd still be wearing this badge."

"True," McKeever said. "I'm a product of a misspent youth, Finley." His glance touched Jim Singleton. "Let this be an example to you, son. Work hard, save your money, and stay away from strong drink, fast women, and cards."

"Oh, cut it out," Fineen said. "McKeever, don't you

ever take anything seriously?"

"Sure. I take you seriously, Finley."

Fineen frowned. "What the hell's that supposed to mean?"

"Finley Fineen, the intrepid lawman," McKeever said. "I always thought of you as a good carriage maker and nothing else. You look different carrying a gun, Finley. You pretty fair on the draw?"

"Don't play games with me, Lincoln. You'll stretch a long-standing friendship out of shape." He looked then at Jim Singleton. "Why don't you go take your big ears for a walk?"

"Huh?" Jim said, startled.

"Lay off the boy, Finley. He's not bothering you."

Fineen's glance returned to McKeever. "I was talking to him, not you. Besides, I've seen you roust plenty of fellows around."

"No one that didn't have it coming," McKeever said flatly. "What do you want, Finley? My beer's getting stale."

"All right," Fineen said. "Be a sorehead because I got your job."

"Sorehead?" Jim piped in. "Hell, he ain't—" Then he caught McKeever's look and closed his mouth.

Fineen said, "Lincoln, I want those metal pieces Leggitt says you're fooling with."

"Don't have 'em."

"What do you mean, you don't have 'em?"

"That's what I said. Someone stole 'em a couple of days ago."

This made Finley Fineen angry and he didn't try to

hide it. "By God, you could have said something to me about it!"

"Well," McKeever said, "you never asked me and I never thought to mention it. Anyway, they got me in trouble with Leggitt and his damned paper. I didn't care either way, if you know what I mean."

"Those pieces were evidence," Fineen said. "Good God, Lincoln, no wonder Leggitt wanted you kicked out, as sloppy as you are." He pushed himself erect. "I don't suppose you have any idea who took 'em?"

"None whatsoever," McKeever said gently. "You think they were important, Finley?" Then he shrugged. "I guess not. But it was fun trying to put 'em together. You now how I like puzzles." Then he switched the subject quickly. "How you coming along with Doc's killing."

"Nowhere," Fineen admitted. "And you're no help to me." He turned and stalked out, banging the doors as he made his exit.

Jim Singleton lowered his voice and said, "How come you lied to him, Lincoln? I never knew you to tell anyone a lie before."

For a moment McKeever sat in silence, his eyes thoughtful. "I don't know, Jim. Ever play hunches? You know, it's funny to me that Finley would take those pieces of brass so seriously. What I mean is, even Doc Harris treated it like a joke; he never could get serious about it or believe they'd lead to anything. Leggitt didn't, and neither did anyone else."

"I did," Jim said.

"Did you really?" McKeever shook his head. "If I

hadn't insisted on you helping Doc you'd have gone home to bed. Isn't that right?"

"Yeah," Jim said. "It's right."

"But Finley's real interested. Makes me wonder why." McKeever stood up, leaving his beer and unfinished game. "Be real interesting to find out, huh, Jim?"

12.

THURSDAY MORNING THE TELEGRAPHER COPIED A message received from the marshal at Woodland concerning the eight thousand dollars turned over to him by the local attorney. The telegrapher took the message to Finley Fineen, and then spread the news all over town.

Lincoln McKeever was at the cemetery, sitting on a small headstone near Doc Harris' grave when Jim Singleton came up, out of breath and full of talk. McKeever listened with quiet attention, and when Jim Singleton finished, McKeever just sighed and stood up.

"For Pete's sake, doesn't this mean anything to you?" Jim demanded. "Some of the money's turned up. This kind of throws your theory into a cocked hat, doesn't it?"

"No," McKeever said softly. "Not yet, Jim."

"What do you mean, not yet?"

"It all depends on what Finley Fineen does," McKeever said. "Go keep an eye on Finley for me, Jim."

"Hell, what am I looking for?"

"See if Finley Fineen leaves town," McKeever said. "If he does—" McKeever shrugged.

"And if not?"

"Then I can assume that Finley has reached the same conclusion I have concerning the whereabouts of the killer, or he knows that the money that turned up in Woodland was sent there as a dodge."

"Gosh," Jim Singleton said. "How could he know a thing like that if he wasn't—"

McKeever's glance cut him off. "Don't say it, Jim. It might slip out when you didn't want it to." He gave the young man a push. "Go on now and keep an eye on Finley Fineen. I'll take it from there."

"All right," Jim said and walked on down the street. . . .

Dal Leggitt was on the porch of the Hanover House with Nan Singleton, and on impulse McKeever went over there. Dal Leggitt stopped talking when McKeever hailed in earshot, then gave him a blunt stare.

"You're not wanted around here, McKeever."

"Oh?" McKeever was the model of mildness. His quick glance went to Nan. "Dal the boss yet?"

"No," Nan said. "I was going to bring out some tea and cake. Care for some, Lincoln?"

"Why, I sure would." He stepped up on the porch and brushed Leggitt's arm aside to pass. "You don't mind, do you, Dal?"

"I do mind. McKeever, I whipped you once. I can put some more marks on your face if that's what you want."

McKeever regarded him solemnly. "What are you going to do after you marry her, Dal? Keep her locked in the closet for fear some man will look sideways at her?" He sat down then and cocked his feet to the railing. "Ahhhh, there's nothing like a good chair." He motioned to a vacant one. "Why don't you sit down, Dal? You look like a dog guarding his dish."

Leggitt hesitated briefly, then sat down. "You know, you don't seem so big without the badge, Lincoln."

"That so?" He glanced at Nan Singleton. "Didn't you say something about tea and cake?"

"Yes, but I was just waiting to see if you two were going to fight again."

"I'm a peaceful man," McKeever said.

"He doesn't like a licking," Leggitt offered. "Isn't that right, Lincoln?"

"If you say so, Dal."

Leggitt stared at McKeever. "You're too damned agreeable."

"Oh? And I guess you're never satisfied. A minute ago you wanted to know if I wanted to fight and now you want to know why I won't."

"I'll get a tray," Nan said and went on inside.

"Happy with your new sheriff?" McKeever asked.

"Anything's an improvement over you," Leggitt said.

"Now you don't mean that, Dal. If I hadn't been engaged to Nan once, you'd think I was a nice guy." He stripped the wrapper from a cigar, then offered one to Dal Leggitt. For a moment it seemed that Leggitt would refuse, then he took it without thanks. "Pretty exciting news, that money turning up in Woodland, huh?"

"Yes," Leggitt said. "I wish I could find Fineen and talk to him about it."

McKeever's interest sharpened. "Where is Fineen?"

"Out to Wade Stanton's place," Leggitt said. "Here's the tea and cake." He got up and made a fuss by taking the tray from Nan Singleton.

"Well, I don't see any blood," Nan said.

"There'll be no trouble," McKeever said. "Now that we all understand which burr's under Dal's blanket." He leaned against the porch railing. "What's Fineen doing out at Wade's place?"

"I don't know," Leggitt said. He glanced at his watch and then slipped it back into his pocket. "Wish he'd get back. I'd like to get some material for next week's paper." His glance touched McKeever. "When are you going to get a job?"

"You're the second man asked me that," McKeever said. "Does my loafing bother you, Dal?"

"It's none of my business what you do," Leggitt said flatly.

"Then why ask?"

Leggitt had an answer, but withheld it, for Finley Fineen drove onto the main street in his buggy. "I'll see you later, Nan," Dal Leggitt said and put his cake dish aside. He dashed off the porch, following Fineen's rig down the street.

"There goes a very busy man," McKeever said. He looked at Nan Singleton. "Aren't you going to argue with me?"

123

"No," she said softly. "Does it give you pleasure to run him down, Lincoln?"

"Maybe I'm as small as Dal," McKeever said. "Might as well be honest, huh? You want to know something? I'm jealous of him."

"You have no right to be," Nan said. "And you made the choice."

"True," McKeever said, rising, setting his cup and plate aside. "I was a fool, Nan. Can you believe it?"

"That you were a fool? Yes, you were. But you don't get a second chance with me, Lincoln. Be sure you understand that."

"Oh, I understand that all right," McKeever said.

He stepped off the porch and walked down the street.

McKEEVER wondered if he wasn't playing a fool's game, just standing around and waiting for something to happen; but then he considered all available facts and decided he had no other choice. There wasn't a man in town he didn't know well, yet at least two of them had banded together to rob and to kill. Two men carried this on their minds day and night. Two men watched themselves to make sure they let nothing slip, made no mistake that would trip them up. To McKeever's way of thinking, this was hardly different from a good stiff game of poker, where a man had to do plenty of close guessing if he expected to end the evening with two dollars in his pocket.

One thing for sure about Dalridge's death, it hadn't been decided and executed on the spur of the moment.

A lot of thinking and a lot of talk had gone into it, not to mention considerable work with the outsized gun and the shell. Time was a factor; a man could spend it, waste it, hoard it, but he couldn't squeeze it or stretch it. Neither could he destroy it. The more McKeever thought of this, the more he became convinced that he was looking for men who had time and a place in common where they could spend time without anyone's ever guessing how it was spent.

McKeever covered his thinking and his searching by hanging around the saloon with a beer glass at his elbow and a deck of cards in front of him. He thought about all these people that he knew so well, especially the ones who always spent a lot of time together. There were those checker games that were played over the feed store Monday and Wednesday nights, but they went right on, same time, same place, same four people. McKeever felt he could rule them out.

During the two days Lincoln McKeever held the town under the magnifying scrutiny of his thoughts, he found that everyone seemed to be going on just as they always did. Kelly and Burgess moved about, making big talk. Sam Richardson made a speech on the saloon porch; he usually made one a week, just to keep himself in the voters' eyes. McKeever began to run out of ideas, and people who shared time together. . . .

The investigator from San Francisco was expected to arrive on Saturday. Everyone was at the stage depot, but he came in on horseback, unnoticed, for he was a thin, stringbean of a man in his late twenties, looking more like a whisky drummer than an insurance detective. He wore a flat-brimmed hat and a serious manner. He put up at the hotel, and had a bath, shave and a haircut in the barbershop before someone happened to look at the hotel register and then realized he had arrived. Then no one remembered what he looked like, except Lincoln McKeever, who had seen him ride in and spotted him right away.

McKeever stayed near the saloon until evening mealtime, then ate in the small restaurant down the street. Around eight he drifted toward Bill Daley's drugstore, bought a few cigars, then paused to pass the time of day with Daley.

"You see the insurance detective yet?"

"Yep," Daley said. "He came in here and bought a package of cough drops, and I didn't even guess who he was."

"Did he ask any questions?"

"Not a damn one, except where was a good place to eat. I told him the Chinese joint on Ash Street."

McKeever was lighting his cigar. "He disappointed some folks, who expected a real two-gun man."

"You want to know something?" Daley said. "People are easily disappointed." He sighed and shook his head.

"I'll walk over to Finley's with you," McKeever said.

Daley looked at him blankly for a moment, then said, "I—I'm not going to play tonight, Lincoln."

"What? Hell, Bill, we've played poker every Sat-

126

urday night for years."

"Count me out tonight," Daley said. "I told Ethel I'd drive her over to her sister's place in Woodland. Figured to stay the weekend."

McKeever went out, scratching his head. Finally he cut across the street to Finley Fineen's office and found the place dark. He banged on the door for a while, then walked back toward the Hanover House, puzzled by the sudden shifting of a familiar routine.

INSIDE the Hanover House, in the dining room, McKeever found Wade and Betty Stanton having dinner. Wade looked around, then said, "You want to sit down, Lincoln?"

"Ah, no," McKeever said. "You going over to Fineen's tonight?"

"We're not playing," Stanton said. "Didn't Finley tell you?"

"No, I guess he forgot about it," McKeever said. "How come, Wade? Someone get sore about something?"

"I don't think so," Stanton said. "Maybe it was Bill's idea. Why don't you ask him?"

"I might," McKeever said.

"Anyhow, it wouldn't be the same without Doc Harris," Stanton said. "I guess it had to break up sooner or later."

"Yeah," McKeever said and walked out.

At his table in the saloon, he laid out his spread of cards and lifted a fresh beer. He kept kicking Stanton's reason around in his mind, trying to get it to settle down, but it seemed as if Harris was reaching out of the grave to upset it every time it started to jell. The more McKeever thought about it, the more troubled he became, until he was forced to start at the beginning again and admit a few things to himself. First, in looking over the town, the quiet gatherings, he had missed one, or had deliberately dismissed it; he wasn't sure which. But the fact remained that he had disregarded the Saturday poker games in Fineen's place.

The thought seemed ridiculous, yet he could not seem to put it aside. Habit was a funny thing, the way it took hold of a man, made him dress a certain way, talk with a certain quaintness, and even think along clearly outlined patterns. Then all of a sudden something changed, without a reason. McKeever could remember plenty of times when a good reason came along to miss a poker session, yet no one had. Then all of a sudden Daley wanted to drive his nagging wife over to her sister's place. And Fineen wouldn't miss his poker; it was the only place in town where he could nip at the bottle without his wife's finding out he'd skipped the pledge. McKeever didn't even know Stanton's excuse, if the man had one; only the fact remained that three men suddenly got tired of playing poker, and all at the same time. If one man had dropped out, McKeever supposed he'd consider that natural, but the excuse of Doc's not being there didn't fit because Doc didn't always show up.

McKeever didn't like to think about time just then, because it made him consider three men who had been his long-time friends in an unholy light. Yet he did think of them, and of the time they spent together when he wasn't around, and all the talk that must have gone on between them. After he had circulated the thought a moment, the rest wasn't so difficult to consider. Instead of two, there was three: Daley, Stanton and Fineen.

The reason for it all was the stickler, and he could think of none. They all had enough money to make most men happy. They had wives and respectability and certainly no criminal pasts, which made all this speculation a little hard to believe. Maybe that's why they did it, it was so completely out of character for them; or better still, all part of a character that had remained hidden.

McKeever disliked the neatness, the ease with which all the pieces went together without one shred of proof, or anything beside his basic suspicion. Fineen could have supplied the buggy, maybe even the gun; Stanton probably drove, and Daley went along because they had to do something with him.

He felt almost a sense of betrayal for thinking these things, yet the feeling was too strong to put down. McKeever didn't know exactly how to go about finding out the truth, but he knew that one of them, if his thinking was right, had gotten scared enough to kill. Maybe he could scare them again.

His hand of solitaire didn't come out, but then he didn't mind since everything else seemed to be falling apart at the seams. He redealt, then looked up in time to see the San Francisco investigator come through the door and head for his table.

An outthrust hand came first, then a brief shake. "I'm Charlie Boomhauer, from San Francisco."

"And you know who I am, or you wouldn't be here," McKeever said. "Quite an entrance you made. The town was disappointed; they expected something more exciting."

"We're both too old to believe in fairy tales," Boomhauer said. "Mr. McKeever, I'll be brief. Just a few questions, if you don't mind. I think it's a relatively simple case and should be cleared up shortly. The crime started in this town, and it'll end here. I cannot see any outside forces at work."

McKeever laid a black queen on a red king. Without taking his attention from the game, he said, "My sentiments exactly, Mr. Boomhauer. What do you want to know?"

13.

THE APPOINTMENT AS SHERIFF GAVE FINLEY FINEEN the license he needed to move around without question, and when he saw Wade Stanton talking to Bill Daley in front of the drugstore, Fineen crossed over. Daley was standing by his new buggy, waiting for a fussing wife; both men turned as Fineen came up in a foul frame of mind.

"The damned gall of Kelly and Burgess. You hear about it?"

"Hear about what?" Stanton asked.

"They turned in a claim to the insurance company of over forty thousand apiece," Fineen said. "Boy, if that ain't crust, I never seen it." He slapped his hands together. "You know, there's a lot of profit in being robbed, when you get it back with interest like that."

Wade Stanton smiled. "Well, Finley, why don't you go tell the insurance investigator. Boomhauer, was that his name?"

"Very funny," Fineen said, scowling. "But it sure gets me, that's all."

"It ought to make you feel good," Bill Daley said. "I mean, now you know that you're not the only crook around Two Pines."

"You could write Boomhauer an anonymous letter and tell him about it," Stanton suggested.

"That would be real smart," Fineen said flatly. "Real smart."

Stanton shrugged. "About as smart as mailing some money to Woodland to make everyone think someone there tried to spend some of it."

"You seem damned sure of that accusation," Fineen snapped back.

"I'm pretty sure," Stanton said. "I know I didn't send it, and Bill's too tight to spend a dollar, so it must have been you. Finley, you'll have to go over to Woodland and fuss around to make this look good."

"Yeah, I'm riding over Monday with Boomhauer." He raised a hand and mopped his face. "McKeever made me jumpier than I thought, but it's all right now."

Daley tipped back his head and looked at the

upstairs windows. "Wonder what's keeping Ethel?"

"You in a hurry to get out of town?" Fineen asked. "I'd hate to think you were going somewhere else to live, Bill."

"You think I'd take her along if I was?" He nodded toward Fineen's shoulder. "Here comes Lincoln Mc-Keever. I can do without him right now."

McKeever had a cigar locked between his teeth, and a smile for them. "Together again," he said smoothly. "What are you doing, Finley? Talking about how to get rid of the money?"

Bill Daley took a deep breath and held it. Stanton's expression froze, but Finley Fineen's remained unchanged. "What the hell you talking about?"

"The money Dalridge was carrying." He pursed his lips briefly. "Come on, Finley, it wasn't so hard to figure out."

"That's a damned serious accusation to make against a man without proof," Stanton said.

McKeever glanced at him, smiling. "Now, you know me, Wade. Do I ever bluff without the cards to back me up? How about it, Finley, you going to cut me in, or do I talk?"

"You're beating the wrong bush this time," Fineen said flatly. "Lincoln, I'm willing to forget you ever said this, but I'll tell you now that if you spread talk about us, I'll kill you."

"You may think that's cheaper than making another split," McKeever said. "I'll give you an hour or two to kick it around."

"I don't need an hour," Fineen snapped.

Lincoln McKeever looked at Stanton and Daley. "You two don't have much to say—especially you, Bill. I always thought you were real touchy, but now you don't seem to care." He rotated the cigar between his lips. "Let's see now, what would you do with the money? You don't trust your wife and you wouldn't take it to a bank. I'll bet you got it stuck away in a jar someplace where you can take it out now and then and count it." He studied Daley's expression while he spoke, then still smiling, he turned to Wade Stanton. "I think you'd bury yours, Wade, because you're a miserly bastard who likes to have things just to be having them, even when they don't do you a damned bit of good. Money or a wife, it wouldn't make much difference."

"You've said too much," Fineen said. "Get away from us, Lincoln."

"In a minute, in a minute," McKeever said. He took out his watch and looked at it. "I'll give you an hour, gentlemen. You name the place. I'll be at Hanover House. Send a boy when you make up your minds."

McKeever turned and walked away, leaving silence behind him.

WADE Stanton spoke first. "I told you that you made too many mistakes, Finley."

"Shut up!"

"How did he know? Daley asked. "How could he know?"

"He's guessing," Fineen said quickly, "nothing more."

133

"You guess that close, you've got a hit," Stanton said softly. "You played poker with him, Daley. Can't you figure it out?"

"What are we going to do?" This was Daley's one concern.

"We're going to do nothing," Fineen said. "Damn it, how many times do I have to tell you that as long as we don't break and run for it we're safe? All right, so McKeever was smarter than I gave him credit for, and so he guessed the truth, but he won't say anything. That was a bluff to make us break."

"He sounded serious to me," Daley said uneasily.

"It was a bluff, I tell you," Fineen insisted. "He don't have one damned thing to go on. Not one damned thing And he won't talk because he hasn't anything to talk about." He took Daley by the arm and shook him slightly. "You go get your woman and drive her to Woodland, just as if nothing happened. By the time you get back, this whole thing will be done with, finished."

"What you going to do, Finley?" This was Daley's question.

"I'm going to meet him in one hour, as he asks. Then I'm going to run a bluff of my own."

"I don't think you can get away with it," Stanton said.

"No? Who asked you, anyway?"

"Maybe if you'd have shut your mouth once in a while instead of doing all the talking we wouldn't be in this spot now," Stanton said. "You've got to run everything, Finley, and always your way."

"Is that the way you feel about it? Then take your share and shift for yourself. And don't come to me when McKeever starts stepping on your toes."

"I'm not scared of McKeever," Stanton said.

Bill Daley interrupted. "Wade, Finley, don't talk like that. We've got to stick together."

"The hell we do," Fineen said. "If Stanton wants out, then he's free to go. I don't want a man around me who doesn't trust me."

"You said yourself that the worst thing that could happen was for us to fight among ourselves," Daley said. "Finley, Wade didn't mean anything by what he sa—"

"Look, Bill, I'll decide what I meant and didn't mean." He looked at Fineen. "The trouble with you, Finley, is that you figure everybody needs you. Well, I don't. I can handle McKeever by myself, and I won't have to ask you for advice either."

"That suits me," Fineen said. "By golly, I've been a man of honor all my life, and I won't let a crook like you call me a fool." He waved his hand. "Go on, Wade. But walk away now, and it's for good."

"Oh, you're getting me all choked up," Stanton said and stalked down the street.

"I can patch this up," Daley said quickly. "Finley, let me go to him and I'll get it all straightened out."

"No," Fineen said, his eyes following Stanton. "I didn't know it until this minute, but I never liked him. Not one damned bit I never."

LINCOLN McKeever waited on the porch of the

Hanover House as he had promised, only he did not wait alone, for Betty Stanton sat close beside him. They talked in low tones and she laughed repeatedly and Nan Singleton, when she brought out the tray of coffee McKeever ordered, set it down a little harder than was necessary.

To anyone passing along the walk, and there were many who noticed, Lincoln McKeever was carrying on an obvious flirtation with Wade Stanton's wife, and she was enjoying every minute of it. McKeever kept a well disguised attention on the street, and saw Wade Stanton approaching on the opposite boardwalk. He stopped at the base of the steps, one hand on the porch rail.

"You two amusing each other?" Stanton asked. Nan Singleton came to the door and Stanton glanced at her, then back to McKeever.

"Your wife is charming company," McKeever said, "but I don't think we'd ever quarrel over that point, would we, Wade?" He eased out of his chair then and stood near Stanton. "Did Fineen send you?"

Wade said, "This is between the two of us."

"What is?"

Wade Stanton glared for a moment, then said, "McKeever, I'm tired of having you fool around my wife."

This was the kind of talk to make people interested, and Wade said it in a voice that would carry. Several men stopped, looked at each other, then decided to remain to see what came next.

"Take this someplace else," Nan Singleton said. "I

run a decent place here."

A few more men attached themselves to the lingering group on the walk, and a crowd attracts a crowd. Within half a minute, twenty-five men stood there, smoking, looking, waiting.

"Wade, you're making a fool of yourself," Betty Stanton said. "And you're embarrassing me."

"Too bad about you," Wade said. "How about it, Lincoln? We going to settle this man to man?"

"If you think there's anything to settle," McKeever said. He smiled thinly. "What are you going to do, Wade? Whip me with a gun barrel?"

"I don't do things that way," Stanton said flatly.

"Well, I didn't think you did," McKeever said softly. "But if it's a fight you want, I'll accommodate you."

"I'm not carrying a gun," Stanton said, "but I'll sure get one."

"Gun? Fineen wants this done permanently, huh?"

"Fineen doesn't give me orders," Stanton said. "This is purely my pleasure." He spun around and went across the street to his buggy. From under the seat he took a cartridge belt and buckled it on. Nan Singleton came out and took McKeever's arm. "You fool, would you fight over her? Kill for her?"

HE wanted to tell her the truth, but he could not, and he knew that if he didn't tell her in this moment, she would never believe it later. "Get back," he said softly. "Take Betty inside."

"No," Nan said. "She wants to see it. She's waited long enough to see it."

A lane opened up for Wade Stanton; he stopped at the walk's edge.

McKeever stood with his hands in his coat pockets. "Wade, you're a damned fool. You haven't got a chance and you know it."

"What kind of a chance will I have if I don't go through with this?"

"All right, you figure it that way if you want," McKeever said. "But there's only one way for you to find out, Wade, and this time it could be with your life, not just a few dollars."

There was a hushed period when both men waited; then Wade Stanton reached for his gun. He wasn't fast, but he was good, and as the barrel came level, his thumb eared back the hammer while Lincoln McKeever remained rooted, his hands in his coat pockets. An instant before Stanton fired, McKeever shot, right through the pocket, leaving a burning eye of cloth. Stanton staggered back and sent his shot into the porch planks. He quickly clasped his left hand over his breast and stared at Lincoln McKeever.

"Damned . . . pea-shooter anyway," he said, and then fell.

The crowd broke, and Lincoln McKeever flogged the pocket of his coat, beating out the smoldering ring. He broke open the .32 and replaced the spent cartridge from the few spares he carried in a pocket. Betty Stanton stood by the rail, staring at her dead husband.

"Now you've got it all," McKeever said softly. "All of that money." He started to turn, then stopped to add,

"Get a shovel and start digging. You might be surprised at how much more you'll find."

Her expression was blank, mirroring her lack of understanding. Then he stepped inside the hotel and looked toward the desk where Nan Singleton stood.

"Well," Nan said, her voice softly bitter, "she finally got you to kill for her, didn't she, Lincoln?"

14.

FINLEY FINEEN HEARD ABOUT THE SHOOTING WITHIN minutes, and the news was like a blow to the face; the fact that Wade Stanton was so quickly dead was almost beyond belief. Evidently Bill Daley thought so too, for he defied his wife by canceling the ride to Woodland.

As Fineen stepped out of his office, he met Daley coming across the street.

"What are you going to do about this?" Daley wanted to know.

"Arrest McKeever," Finley Fineen said. "What the hell can I do?"

"Did you ever think that maybe he wanted to be arrested?"

"Yes, I thought of that. It's a chance I have to take," Fineen said. "God, you're not going to get as nervous like Wade was, are you?"

"No," Daley said. He put his hand to his face. "Finley, I've got to get out of here. Go to Arizona. Ethel can have the place. I'll take my share and—"

"You spend one cent of that money and I'll kill you," Fineen said.

Daley backed up a step. "Now hold on there. You sent that lawyer in Woodland eight thousand dollars. That wasn't in the damn plan."

"Neither was killing Doc Harris!" Fineen calmed himself. "Let's not start pulling apart, Bill. Wade did, and got himself killed for it."

"McKeever's got to be shut up some way," Daley said. "I mean it, Finley. He's dangerous."

"You don't have to tell me about McKeever." Fineen wiped a hand across his mouth. "I'd better get over to the hotel before someone sends for me. I want to talk to McKeever alone."

"Don't let him get your goat," Daley warned. "That's his game, getting us to do something foolish, and Wade fell for it."

"Don't keep telling me stuff I already know!"

He wheeled away, toward the hotel. Several men were carrying Wade Stanton away when he arrived. Charlie Boomhauer was there, his face more grave than usual.

"Where's McKeever?" Fineen asked, speaking to anyone who would answer him.

One man nodded toward the inside. "In there."

Fineen went in and found McKeever in the lobby, alone. As Fineen came up, McKeever took his watch from his pocket and consulted it. "I thought you'd get here sooner than this," he said.

"I want to talk to you, alone," Fineen said.

"We're alone here," McKeever said.

140

"Let's take one of the empty rooms," Fineen said. "And keep your damned hands out of your coat pockets."

"You arresting me?"

"We'll talk first," Fineen said. "Come on."

FINEEN went behind the counter, snagged a key off the hook and led the way down the hall. He unlocked the door and went on in to light the lamp. Then he closed the door and locked it before speaking. "Wade was a fool. I told him I'd handle it."

"Yeah, he was a fool. So you handle it."

Fineen said, "What am I going to do with you, Lincoln?"

"I was waiting for you to figure it out," McKeever said. "I don't think the judge will hold me. Too many witnesses to the shooting. You see, I had the drop on Wade and told him so, but he drew anyway. I had to shoot in self-defense."

"You're damned smart," Finley Fineen said. "I wish to God you were stupid." He sat down then and studied his huge hands.

"How did it ever get started, Finley? You know, talking about it?"

He looked up quickly, then laughed. "Why shouldn't I tell you? If you repeated it I'd call you a liar."

"Did you think of it first?"

"No," Fineen said softly. "I think Bill Daley did. You know how he is, sometimes. Full of big talk." Fineen shook his head. "I've thought about it a lot, Lincoln, how it worked up from just talk to—"

"—to murder?"

"It didn't start out that way," Fineen said quickly. "We kept kicking the idea around just to have something different to talk about, I guess. Lincoln, didn't you ever get tired of this damned town, and the same people and the same conversations all the time?"

"Yes, but never that tired."

"Then we're not alike," Fineen said. "Hell, I go home at night and Madge says, 'How did it go today?' Every night for eleven years it's the same damned question."

"And the same answer, Finley?"

"Huh?"

"What do you say in answer?"

He thought a moment. "I say, 'Fine. Just fine.' "

"Maybe you ought to have brought your wife in on this too, Finley. She'd have the same reason as you."

Fineen looked at McKeever. "You want me to confess? Say I'm sorry?"

"No, you're not sorry, Finley. You're not sorry because underneath all that good will and fine citizenship you're nothing but a thief and a killer. I think you enjoyed beating Dalridge's brains out with a gun barrel. I think you've always wanted to beat someone's brains out." Fineen started to get up, but McKeever's voice drove him back. "Sit down! I'll tell you when you can get up. Finley, you know and I know all about this. And you know I can't even open my mouth about it because everyone would laugh at me; I couldn't prove a thing. But I want to tell you something. You and I are going to play a little game. Bill Daley's in it too, because I think he killed Doc

Harris; you wouldn't have done such a messy job of it. This little game is for keeps, Finley, like the one I played with Wade Stanton. I'm going to hound you until I make you break and run. And when you do, it'll be out in the open and then every peace officer west of the Mississippi will join in with me. It's going to be a grand hunt, Finley. You, me, and Bill Daley. I'll never let up on you, so watch yourself." Then he went to the door and flung it open. "Get out of here. And don't make any mistakes, Finley."

Finley Fineen sat in the chair, sweat bold on his forehead. He said, "Suppose I drew on you now, Lincoln?"

"Too late," McKeever said, turning so that Fineen could see the pocket that had a moment ago been hidden from sight; McKeever's hand was in it, and Fineen understood what that meant. "A thirty-two is small, but it does the job." He nodded again toward the open door. "All right, now get going."

Fineen got up and stepped to the hall. "Lincoln, you chose the odds, two against one."

"You're scared, Finley. How do you sleep at night? Do you ever worry about talking in your sleep?" His smile was mocking.

Spinning on his heel, Finley Fineen walked rapidly down the hall, then took the stairs two at a time. McKeever blew out the lamp and locked the door before returning to the lobby. He rehung the key, then on impulse he turned toward the kitchen.

He saw Dal Leggitt first, seated at the table, then

when McKeever stepped deeper into the room he saw Nan Singleton, her back toward him. When she turned around to see who it was he noticed that her eyes and nose were red from crying.

"Get out of here," Leggitt said bitterly. "McKeever, you spoil everything you touch."

"Why don't you just shut your mouth for a while," McKeever said.

Nan took a final sniff, a final dab with the handkerchief and said, "Betty's at her father's house. Why don't you go there, Lincoln? Don't stand on formality now."

"Nan," McKeever said, "I wish you'd listen to me."

"She doesn't have to listen to you," Leggitt said. "I told her time and time again how this would end; maybe now she'll believe me." He got up and put his arm around her, but she shrugged off his embrace.

"Just leave me alone, Dal."

"With him?"

This made her angry. "Oh, don't be stupid!"

He was easily offended. Taking up his hat, he stepped to the door. "Very well, Nan. When you come to your senses, call me."

When Leggitt's footfalls faded, McKeever said, "Nan, will you listen to me?"

"No," she said. "I meant you too when I said I wanted to be left alone." She faced him quickly. "Oh, Lincoln, I wish I hated you."

He had no words for her, no ready explanation; he went out and paused on the boardwalk. From the shadows of the porch, Charlie Boomhauer spoke.

"Got a minute, McKeever?"

"Sure. Here?"

"No," Boomhauer said. "Let's walk."

He fell in beside McKeever and they started down the street, Boomhauer remaining silent until they came to the residential district.

"How much money do you think the robbers got?" Boomhauer asked.

"Don't you know?"

"I know what Mr. Kelly and Mr. Burgess claim was stolen," he said, "but I haven't had a chance to check it. Those things take time, you know. I'll have to audit all the accounts listed in their books, then check the balance owed against their claim."

"Why ask me?"

"Because you know this town. And because you were the sheriff when this happened." Boomhauer paused to light a cigar, and then he walked on, his step slow and even. "That quarrel you had with Wade Stanton—was that as personal as it looked?"

"No," McKeever said. "But I couldn't prove anything."

"That's often the case," Boomhauer admitted. "I'm interested in finding the money and absolving my company of a large claim payment. Catching killers I leave to marshals and sheriffs. You follow me?"

"Maybe I do," McKeever said. "You want me to go ahead with what I'm doing, and you'll follow along to pick up the pieces. Is that it?"

Boomhauer chuckled. "That's the general idea, as long as the pieces are money." He paused to draw on his smoke. "This Stanton, was he in on the robbery?"

"Yes, he and two others."

"Suppose you name them to me."

"I'll name Stanton. The other two I'll deal with my own way. As you said, Boomhauer, there's murder connected with this. And that's my department."

"It's the law's department. And you're not the law."

"There are times," McKeever said, "when the individual must be the law."

FOR a time Boomhauer said nothing, then he posed a question. "Are you going to make me hunt the money that was Stanton's share? Or are you going to tell me where it is?"

"I don't know where it is," McKeever said.

Charlie Boomhauer chuckled. "McKeever, you were smart enough to put this together so far. I assume you're smart enough to take it the rest of the way. Where do you think the money is hidden?"

"Go buy a shovel," McKeever said.

Boomhauer threw his cigar into the street. "I believe I will. And it's been pleasant talking to you."

When he turned to leave, McKeever took his arm. "There might be others digging."

"I'll enjoy the company," Boomhauer said.

Lincoln McKeever laughed. "Nothing much bothers you, does it?"

"No," Boomhauer said. "I think that's a trait we share in common. And incidentally, if you settle with the other two as finally as with Stanton, will you please bear in mind my interest in the money?"

"Yes," McKeever said. "That won't be difficult."

Boomhauer headed back toward the central part of town, and Lincoln McKeever remained under the trees.

The shot came as a complete surprise, a carnation of flame and an echo that slapped among the quiet houses. McKeever assumed that the bullet was meant for him and pulled his pistol from his pocket, but before he could even aim it in the general direction of the assailant, Boomhauer had his .44 free of the shoulder holster and was rolling a cylinder full of lead at the trees twenty yards beyond.

This sudden volley was enough to make the trees untenable, and a man quickly dashed down the street, his steps spanking the boardwalk. McKeever started to race after him, but Boomhauer called him back.

"No use, McKeever. The night's dark and there're too many alleys down there to duck into. Hell, he could hide behind someone's rosebush and you'd walk right by him while he aimed at your back."

Booomhauer was punching the empties from his gun and after he reloaded it, he replaced it in the holster.

"I didn't know you were carrying that," McKeever said.

Boomhauer smiled. "I just look innocent."

Lights popped on and a few people stuck their heads out of upstairs windows, but after a moment they ducked back inside, convinced it was all over.

"Whoever it was, his aim was sure lousy," McKeever said.

"Really?" Boomhauer lifted the tail of his coat and poked a finger through the hole. "It seems, McKeever, that we have more than one thing in common. We are alike in appearance just enough so that in poor light, I could be mistaken for you, and you for me."

"Come on," McKeever said. "I owe you a drink."

"And a needle and thread," Boomhauer said.

15.

AT NINE O'CLOCK THE NEXT MORNING, THE JUDGE held an inquest and heard witnesses testify that Lincoln McKeever was justified in shooting Wade Stanton, since Stanton had picked the quarrel and then tried to draw against the drop. The verdict was not difficult to reach and McKeever walked out twenty minutes later, Charlie Boomhauer at his elbow. They walked down the street to the saloon, ordered two glasses of beer, then went to McKeever's favorite table.

Boomhauer said, "This newspaperman, Leggitt, he's going to stir up all the feeling against you he can."

"I expect that."

"You changed your mind yet and decided to work along with me?"

"I'd like to work with you," McKeever said, "but you'll have to do your job your way and let me do mine my way."

"That sounds reasonable," Boomhauer said mildly. "I don't think we'll get in each other's way."

"I think Bill Daley and Finley Fineen are the other two we want."

Boomhauer's eyes widened. "Fineen? Why, he's the sheriff!"

"He wasn't sheriff then," McKeever said. "Look, Charlie, you've got to go along with me, all the way. Either I have that or you can figure it out for yourself."

"Just give me something to go on," Boomhauer said. "I'm a reasonable man."

Lincoln McKeever did. He outlined his way of thinking, and one by one, pointed out the conclusions he had reached. Boomhauer was quick-witted and ready to find fault, but there was none. Because he knew these men, and this town, he had arrived at some startling answers.

"All right," Boomhauer said, when McKeever finished. "I'll buy it, McKeever. But where do we go from here?"

"I think you'd better get a restraining order from the court to keep Betty Stanton's hands off Wade's property. At least until you have time to look for the money."

"That won't be difficult. And you?"

"Well, Bill Daley is the weak link, so I'm going to start to lean on him and see if I can break him off at the ankles."

Charlie Boomhauer raised his coat and indicated the bullet hole. "Don't forget this, McKeever. Either of them will kill you if they get the chance." He hunched forward. "If you were killed, I couldn't do a thing about it. There's no evidence against them now, and if

Fineen is running this, as you say, he's smart enough to make sure no one drops anything." He shook his head. "Your way's pretty risky, McKeever. I'd advise against it."

"I didn't ask for that. You said you'd go along."

"And I won't go back on it," Boomhauer said. "Do you have a plan?"

McKeever admitted, "The way I figure it, if Fineen and Daley sit tight, we'll never get anything on them, and my accusation won't mean a thing if I can't prove it." He rubbed a hand across his face. "My only chance is to make one of them break, and that would be Daley. I think he got scared enough once to kill Doc Harris, and I'm going to scare him again."

"He knows you're on to him," Boomhauer pointed out. "And he'll know what you're trying to do. McKeever, I don't think it's going to work."

"Yes it is," McKeever said, then leaned forward to tell why in little more than a whisper. Boomhauer listened with a quickened interest, then he slapped the table and laughed. "Well?" McKeever asked. "How about it?"

"I think so," Boomhauer said. He scraped his chair back. "I'd better get that restraining order. Good luck, McKeever."

AFTER he left, McKeever had a refill on his beer, then played solitaire until noon. One of the town barflies mooched two drinks off McKeever, then he sent the man on an errand.

Ten minutes later Jim Singleton came in and sat

down. "You wanted to see me?"

"Like to do a job tonight? It might be risky."

Jim Singleton didn't hesitate. "Sure. You name it."

McKeever did. "Spend the night in my room. Keep the lamp going until around midnight, then lock the door and go to bed."

"That's risky?"

"Someone took a shot at me last night," McKeever said. "They may try it again."

Jim Singleton swallowed hard. "Can I have a gun to shoot back?"

"There's a rifle and a box of shells in my room," McKeever said. "Jim, I want you to stay in that room until I tell you to come out."

"Yes, sir."

"All right," McKeever said. "Sneak in right after dark, and make sure the lamp is on."

Jim Singleton nodded. "Can I tell Nan?"

"God, no! Look, keep this to yourself."

"What you up to, Lincoln?"

"I wouldn't say," McKeever told him. "Go on now."

He killed the afternoon by loafing in the saloon. That evening, when he went to the restaurant he met Dal Leggitt having an early supper. In passing Leggitt's table, McKeever said, "How come you're not over to Nan's place sponging a free meal?"

This drew a frown across Leggitt's forehead. "Sit down, McKeever. I want to talk to you."

After a moment's hesitation, McKeever took the chair across from him. He gave his order to the waiter; then McKeever said, "What's on your mind, Dal?"

"What to do about you," Leggitt said.

"I didn't know you could do anything about me," McKeever said.

Leggitt speared a piece of steak with his fork and chewed violently. "McKeever, you're the worst thing that ever happened to this town. If I ever needed proof, I had it when you shot Wade Stanton down in cold blood."

"You're doing a lot of guessing there," McKeever said. "Dal, you don't even know what's going on around here. All you ever think about is yourself. That lousy little paper of yours is just a showcase for your own small-minded opinions."

Leggitt was quietly angry; his eyes took on a brilliant sheen. "Lincoln, that lousy little paper, as you call it, is just big enough to run you out of town. That's my ambition now."

"Well, it's growing, anyway," McKeever said. His supper arrived and he began to eat. "At first you were just interested in bucking me when I ran for sheriff. Then you decided you'd grown enough to throw me out of office by getting Kelly and Burgess stirred up."

"And now I'm big enough to push you all the way out of town," Dal Leggitt said. "Why don't you go out to Stanton's place and live with Betty? I wouldn't want to think you killed Wade for nothing."

McKeever's first impulse was to hit him, but he had too much to lose by embroiling himself with Dal Leggitt.

And Leggitt was the kind who would mistake

judgment for cowardice. He placed his hands on the table and said, "You're yellow, McKeever."

Now that the first shock of anger passed, McKeever was almost amused by Leggitt. The man was like a small boy approaching a strange dog, timidly at first, then with increasing boldness. McKeever believed that a sudden, move on his part would make Leggitt jump.

But McKeever did none of these things. He merely shrugged and went on eating, unmindful of the other diners who were listening to every word said.

Dal Leggitt found something more interesting than food, a person he could torment and get away with it. "Your presence here offends me," he said. "Get up and get out of this restaurant while I'm eating my supper."

Even the dishwasher stopped and came to the kitchen door to see this. Lincoln McKeever wiped his lips with his napkin and slowly stood up. Someone gasped and someone else groaned while Dal Leggitt smiled.

McKeever took Leggitt's plate from the table and set it on the floor. Then he looked at Leggitt and said, "That's where the dogs eat. Get down there."

For an instant Leggitt just stared and wondered how this could have happened, and what he was going to do about it. He found out when McKeever hit him, driving him out of his chair. Before Leggitt could clear the buzzing from his head, McKeever grabbed him by the hair and pushed his face down to the plate.

Leggitt clawed and tried to fight back, but Mc-

Keever's anger was too strong, his strength too determined now. Hauling Leggitt erect, McKeever shoved him toward the front door while potatoes and peas and gravy dribbled off Leggitt's face. Not bothering to open the door, McKeever merely drove Leggitt against it with enough force to carry away the hasp; then they were crossing the walk and Leggitt was propelled by McKeever's foot into the street. He struck and rolled and then sat up, stunned, shamed, afraid to get up.

"You want me to wait?" McKeever said. "Come on, Dal, you wanted trouble. Here's a big bundle of it." He stepped toward Leggitt. "Show me how a dog walks, Dal. Go on, show me!" He gave Leggitt a kick to get him started.

On hands and knees, Leggitt started to move away, but McKeever stepped up and grabbed him by the collar, hauling him back. Leggitt struck at McKeever's legs and earned a clout on the ear for his trouble. The crowd had come outside the restaurant to see this and all the business houses along the street hurriedly emptied.

"See that hitching post over there? Go over and show everyone how a dog takes a leak," McKeever said. "Damn you, Dal, you'd better do it!"

"Ain't he had enough?" one man asked.

McKeever's glance whipped around and singled this man out. "*I've* had enough. You want to join him?"

"I was just sayin'," the man murmured and fell silent.

Leggitt was still on his hands and knees, head

raised, watching McKeever. "Let me up and I'll fight you," Leggitt said.

"You like to fight with your mouth," McKeever said. "Get over to that post."

"I won't do it," Leggitt said dully. "You do what you want, but I won't do it." He raised a hand to mingle dust with the food still stuck to his face. "Let me have a gun, somebody. For God's sake, let me have a gun!"

McKeever waited, then a man spoke up. "How about it, McKeever? You want me to give him mine?"

"Do as you damned please," McKeever said.

The man hesitated, then took a long-barreled .45 from his waistband. "A man ought to have the right to settle a thing anyway he wants." He tossed the gun into the dust by Leggitt's knee.

"Well?" McKeever said and stood there.

Leggitt looked at the gun for a long moment, then raised his eyes to Lincoln McKeever. "You want to chalk up another killing, don't you?"

"No," McKeever said. "But I'll let you start anything you think you can finish."

LEGGITT's hand came out briefly and almost touched the gun, but then he started to shake. Suddenly he clasped both hands over his face and rocked forward on his elbows and knees. The man who had tossed the gun stepped forward and picked it up.

The crowd seemed to melt then and McKeever turned back inside the restaurant to finish his meal. One man stopped by his table and said, "You'd have been a lot kinder if you'd just shot him, Lincoln. Dal's

155

through in Two Pines. Won't be anyone who'll listen to anything he has to say from now on."

"Yes," McKeever said, somewhat sadly. "Remember that when you feel like talking too much."

His meal ended, McKeever paid the counter man and went out. At the stable he rented a horse and a saddle, then went to his room and changed clothes. He slipped into a pair of levis and a tan canvas brush jacket. From the bureau drawer he took a worn .38-40 with belt and holster and buckled this around his waist.

When the door opened he turned quickly, then relaxed when Jim Singleton stepped into the room. The young man's face was serious. "Heard what happened to Dal. I wouldn't go near Nan for a while if I was you."

"I don't intend to," McKeever said. "That's the part I don't like, what she's thinking."

"You done that awful hard," Jim said. "Nan says too hard. Dal didn't have it coming."

"I thought he did," McKeever said.

"Sure, I understand all right." He nodded toward McKeever's worn clothes. "Never seen you in anything but a suit before, Lincoln."

"I wore these clothes when I came to Two Pines."

"You leavin'?" Jim asked.

"For a while," McKeever said. "I'll go out the back window. You sure no one saw you come in?"

"No, I sneaked in. Where you going?"

McKeever shook his head. "I'll be back. Remember

what I said about the lamp, and stay here until I tell you to leave." Then he opened the window and left.

16.

LINCOLN MCKEEVER DIDN'T OFTEN GET TO WOODland, at least not more than two or three times a year. The town was built on the flats, which extended on for nearly eight miles before they were broken up by low rolling hills. This was cattle country, rough country, with a man's nearest neighbor ten or twelve miles away. The men here were loners, and they liked it that way.

Riding down the main street, McKeever stopped at the saloon, for at a quarter to three in the morning, only the saloon stayed open. He tied his horse and went inside. A sleepy bartender racked glasses while a long-winded poker game went on in one corner.

"Whisky," McKeever said, and then with his drink paid for, he felt free to venture the next question. "Marshal Green around?"

"Went to bed two hours ago," the bartender said.

"He still sleeping in the office?"

"Yeah," the bartender said. "Say, ain't you the sheriff from Two Pines? Didn't recognize you without your suit on."

McKeever lingered a moment longer, then went out and down the dark street. The marshal's office and two-by-four jail sat near an alley and McKeever pounded on the oak door until he heard Green's outraged voice: "All right, all right, I'm coming!"

A lamp was lighted, then Green flung the door open and thrust his belligerent face and a pistol at McKeever. "What the blue blazes you want? That you, McKeever? Come on in." He put the pistol down and hitched up his suspenders. "Couldn't it wait until morning?"

You sleep until noon anyway," McKeever said. "I came after that money, Ben."

"The eight thousand? It's in Lon Beasley's safe."

"I'd like to get it tonight," McKeever said.

"Well, Lon ain't going to like being got out of bed," Ben Green said. "You can't wait, huh?"

"I'm going back as soon as I can get a fresh horse."

"All right," Green said and put on his shirt and hat. He sat down on the edge of his cot to wrestle on his boots, then blew out the lamp and walked three blocks south with Lincoln McKeever.

Lon Beasley took his time about answering the door, but his annoyance vanished when he saw who it was. He shook hands with McKeever and said, "I expected you before this, Sheriff."

"Been pretty busy," McKeever admitted. "If I can sign for the money, I'll be on my way so you can get back to bed."

"Hell, the damage has been done," Beasley said. "I'm awake now. Care for a drink?"

"Had one at the saloon," McKeever said.

Beasley shrugged. "Have a chair. I'll go get the money."

After he left the room, Green said, "Been thinking

about that money, Lincoln. Seems damned funny a man would send an amount like that through the mails. Especially when he was so careless as to leave a strip of the binder that made identification easy."

"He wanted you to identify it," McKeever said. "I'm getting pretty close to my man, Ben. But I need this money because there's an insurance investigator from San Francisco snooping around and he's getting real nervous because it isn't where he can put his hands on it."

"Don't blame him," Green said. "A man could take eight thousand and live out his life in Mexico. Live damned good too."

Lon Beasley came back with the money. "You want to count it, Lincoln?"

"No, just wrap it in some paper and put a string around it."

"Trusting soul," Beasley said and bound the bills tightly.

"Can I rent a fast horse here?" McKeever asked of Green.

"I've got a bay you can have, but she's a little spooky yet."

"Can she travel? I want to get back to Two Pines by noon."

Beasley looked up. "Trying to set a record?"

"Trying to get back before I'm missed," McKeever said.

The good-byes were brief, and McKeever went to the stable with the marshal, the package under his arm. Saddled, he stepped aboard and swung out of town, letting the bay work off her ginger.

BEN Green hadn't been stretching the truth any; the bay had heart and all the staying power a man could ask for. He stopped now and then, to rest himself more than the horse, and for over a mile he walked in an attempt to restore some of the feeling into his legs.

Dawn pushed over the rim of the land and he figured up the miles traveled, subtracting them from the total, and found himself nearly an hour ahead of what he had figured.

At ten-thirty he sighted Two Pines, and ten minutes later he was easing through all the back streets to his own room, taking the back window for an entrance.

Jim Singleton was asleep on the bed; he jerked awake, rifle flourished when McKeever's boot rapped the dresser. "Hold it," McKeever said, and saw Jim's face go slack with relief.

There was broken glass on the floor; this crunched beneath McKeever's boots. A bullet pucker dimpled the opposite wall. "You had company, I see."

"Twice," Jim Singleton said. "Man, was I scared!"

"Did you, shoot back?"

"Yeah, but I didn't hit anything."

"It's just as well," McKeever said. He took off his hat and jumper.

"Where the devil you been?" Jim Singleton asked. "Kelly and Burgess were here looking for you."

This filled McKeever with alarm. "You didn't let 'em in, did you?"

"Hell no," Jim said. "I figured you wanted to hide,

160

so I just gave 'em a growl and told 'em if they didn't get the hell away I'd shoot through the door."

Lincoln McKeever smiled. "Good boy, Jim. Were they sore?"

"I'll say. Kelly was cussin' you a blue streak."

"He'll get over it," McKeever said. "Jim, I want you to leave now. Walk up and down the main street twice."

"Huh?"

"Now you just do as I tell you. Stop on the corners and loaf a few minutes, and when you're through, go on home."

"Nan'll be scalding mad. What'll I tell her?"

"Tell her you stayed with me last night."

"She won't like that."

McKeever smiled and pushed him toward the door. "She'll get over it, the same as Kelly and Burgess." He took and set the rifle in the corner, and after Jim left, he swept up the broken glass. He waited then, but not long, no more than a half hour. A knock gently rattled his door and McKeever drew his gun. "Who is it?"

"Charlie Boomhauer."

McKeever opened the door and Boomhauer stepped quickly inside. He smiled. "As soon as I saw Jim, I knew you were back. Did you get the money?"

"Yes. Did you get a restraining order?"

Boomhauer nodded. "Mrs. Stanton is fit to be tied. She wants to see you right away."

"She'll have to wait. Did you bring paper, pen and some ink?"

"Got it right here," Boomhauer said, taking the items from his pocket. He saw the package. "That the money? Boy, if the home office ever finds out I'm going along with you on this, I'll be looking for another job—after I get out of jail." He shook his head. "I've been asking myself why I let you talk me into this. You know I'm supposed to impound all money that was stolen until the case is closed."

"You impound that, and you'll never close the case."

Boomhauer held up both hands. "I'm sold, I'm sold."

"You'd better write the notes," McKeever said. "My hand's pretty well known around town."

"Who'll I start out with?" Boomhauer said, uncorking the ink bottle.

McKeever thought a moment, then said, "Make one out to Cris Meyer, the stableman."

"How much and for what?"

"A new harness, say. Make it expensive, at least two hundred dollars, and specify a lot of silver work." He frowned. "Maybe he'd better have another horse too, a blooded animal. Add another five hundred to that and have Meyer send to Kentucky for a real fine animal."

"You sure can spend someone else's money," Charlie Boomhauer said. He wrote the note, then opened the package of stolen money and put in the right amount before sealing it.

There were other notes to write, to the tailor for clothes, nearly four hundred dollars' worth. The watchmaker was given two hundred for the finest watch and gold fob. And Huddleton, who sold some jewelry, was paid five hundred dollars for a diamond ring to be ordered from Kansas City.

The list was long, for McKeever had an active imagination, and, as Boomhauer said, he was spending someone else's money, a delightful position for any man to be in.

Finally Boomhauer called a halt to it. "You've spent nearly three thousand, Lincoln; let's call it quits. What's this luggage for?"

"In case our friend wants to take a trip," McKeever said and picked up his hat. "You see that those are quietly delivered. I'm going out to Betty Stanton's place."

"All right," Boomhauer said. "Where will you be when the fireworks start?"

"In the saloon where I can keep an eye on things."

"I'll see you there then," Boomhauer said and tucked the letters into his pocket. He smiled and picked up the rest of the money. "You don't mind if I keep this, do you?"

"Not at all. I never use the stuff."

Boomhauer grinned and let himself out. Lincoln McKeever waited for a few minutes, then used the window again. Mounted on the bay, he cut along the back streets to the road out to Wade Stanton's place.

His good sense told him not to go, but then he knew Betty and didn't want her to kick up a needless fuss before Boomhauer and a crew could search for Wade's share of the money. . . .

The four paid hands were lounging near the bunkhouse door when McKeever rode into the yard. One of them, the foreman, came over as he was tying up his horse.

"Wade was a good man. You didn't have to kill him."

McKeever looked at him steadily. "What should I have done?"

The front door opened and Betty came out. "Eddie, go mind your own damned business! Come in, Lincoln. It's been hell, alone like this."

"I thought you liked it alone," McKeever said, entering the house.

She poured a drink for him, and one for herself. "I wanted you to shoot him, Lincoln. And I'm glad you did."

"You've got a surprise coming," McKeever said. "I didn't shoot him because of you, Betty."

She regarded him, surprised. "Well, I guess it isn't too important, is it? Do you know what that Boomhauer did to me? He had a restraining order slapped on the place. I can't even draw a damned dime of Wade's money out of the bank."

"Why don't you hire a lawyer?"

"With what? If I didn't have credit at the stores, I couldn't eat. Lincoln, you don't know how tight-fisted Wade was with a dollar."

"Oh, I know." He downed his drink and put the glass aside. "Why don't you get out for a while, Betty? Oh, yeah, no money. Well, would you take a loan from me?"

From her smile, her relief, he knew that this was what she wanted to see him about, to put the bite on him, and every instinct told him to tell her to go to the devil.

"Lincoln, would you?" She came to him and touched his arms, then pressed against him. "Darling, I knew I could count on you."

He eased away from her, gently. "How much?"

"Four hundred?" Her voice was timid. "I know it's a lot, but after this is cleared up, you'll get it back, and more."

"That'll be something to look forward to," he said. "All right, Betty. You come into town tonight and I'll have it for you."

"I'll pack," she said. "I think I'll go to Cheyenne. Would you come to me in a week or so?"

"Why not?" He smiled. "We can figure something out from there, huh?"

"It won't be difficult, Lincoln. I know it won't."

She walked with him to the door. He stopped and said, "I wouldn't worry about the restraining order if I were you. Once Boomhauer leaves Two Pines, the judge will lift it for you."

"I think I'll sell the place. How much will it bring?"

He made a hasty guess. "Eighteen thousand, I suppose, for a quick sale. Wade must have more than a little put away besides."

She laughed then, for the thought of so much money pleased her. "We can live pretty high on that, Lincoln."

"High enough anyway," he said and stepped off the

porch to his horse. "If you want to pay the men off, I'll tell your father at the bank to take it out of my account. We can add that to the four hundred."

She touched his cheek with her hand. "Dear Lincoln. I owe you so much. And I always pay. You know that, Lincoln, don't you?"

17.

THE LAST PERSON LINCOLN MCKEEVER WANTED TO see was Nan Singleton, yet from the way she waited on the Hanover House porch, McKeever knew that she was waiting for him. He dismounted and tied his horse. Nan said, "Come in, Lincoln. I want to talk to you."

He followed her inside and into her room off the lobby. She closed the door then moved around, her manner restless. "I had a lot of things to say, Lincoln, but now I don't know where to start."

"Start anywhere," he invited. "Maybe we can rearrange the pieces afterward."

"All right, suppose we do it that way then. I thought there was kindness in you, Lincoln. And understanding."

"I take it we're going to talk about Dal Leggitt?"

"That's right. Dal Leggitt."

"Then what's there to talk about? If you love the man, then hate me for making him small and let it go at that."

She looked steadily at him, no longer angry. "Lincoln, I don't love him and you know it. If I had loved him, I don't think you would have treated him like that."

"He got what he asked for," McKeever said. "If you want me to say I'm sorry, you're wasting your time, Nan."

"I don't expect you to be sorry," she said. "Lincoln, if everyone got what they had coming, we'd all be so bruised and battered we couldn't walk." She made a brief fan of her hands. "Maybe we'd better forget it, after all. What will it settle?"

"A long-standing quarrel between us," he said. "Nan, you said that if everyone got their lumps we'd all be pretty bruised and battered. All right, I agree, but at the same time, if everyone tried to even up all the hurt they'd known, they'd be hitting everyone. Once I threw you over for another woman, but if you remember I came here and told you to your face, not meaning to hurt you at all. And since then you've been getting back at me, one way or another. Leggitt wasn't much of a man, just a poodle dog for you. Did you enjoy seeing him fight over you, Nan?"

"You have no right to say that to me!"

"And what right do you think you have, waiting on the porch like some irate wife? Damn it, Nan, people would think we'd been married ten years the way you take me to task all the time."

Color came to her cheeks and she looked away from him. "Does—does it really look like that, Lincoln?"

"You know it does, and you like it." He put his hat aside and stepped up to her. "Now I'll tell you one thing, Nan, it's going to stop. If you want to fight with me, then marry me."

"You don't love me," she said.

"No? Nan, how can you be so sure of everything? When I shot Wade you were so sure it was over Betty. You still think so, don't you?"

"I don't know," she admitted. "I really don't, Lincoln. But I wish I could hate you. It'd make life a lot easier."

"Nan, I'm going to give you some time. Not much, but a little anyway. Then I'm going to ask you once more. If you marry me, I'll stay. If not, I'll move on and get out of your life." He picked up his hat and put it on. "There are a lot of things in this world that'll dazzle a man and Betty was one of them. I'm the kind of a guy who won't guarantee a thing, Nan. If you marry me, I won't promise not to look at another woman or to give up beer and cards. Don't marry me to make me over; I wouldn't do that to you."

He went out then and paused on the porch. Boomhauer exited from the saloon and teetered on the walk's edge, a cigar fragrantly ignited. McKeever crossed over. "Anything stirring?"

"Give it time," Boomhauer said softly. "You see Stanton's wife?"

"Yes," McKeever said and told him what had happened.

"You'd better make the arrangements at the bank, then."

"All right."

Sam Richardson was a little on the unfriendly side,

since Lincoln McKeever had made a widow out of his daughter, and his frown was thunderous when McKeever told him why he wanted to draw out the money. Richardson completed the transaction and McKeever returned to the saloon to wait. Charlie Boomhauer was already there and he shuffled the deck of cards for the first of endless games of double solitaire.

ETHEL Daley began her shopping at eleven, leaving her order with the grocer, who would send the delivery boy around with it later in the day. She had money and everyone knew it, but she never spent much of it, keeping the merchants' favor only by the veiled promise that someday she might spend some of it.

Finley Fineen watched her move along the street; his doorway was a vantage point from which he could observe the town. He saw nothing to arouse his interest until Ethel Daley hurried back toward the drugstore, her step firm and rapid, an unusual pace for a woman who liked to live life leisurely. Fineen watched her ascend the stairs, and a moment later the argument started, loud enough and violent enough to raise heads along the street.

Expecting this to be one of those quick-tempered storms, Fineen waited a few minutes for the quiet he knew would come, but there was none. Ethel Daley was wound up and now Fineen detected the crashing of dishes, the ring of a hurled pot. Amid this sound came Daley's pained yelp, proof of his wife's accuracy.

Leaving his doorway, Fineen moved on down the street, idly curious as to what had set this off. He stopped when the saddlemaker came out of his shop, plainly eager for talk. The saddlemaker nodded toward the drugstore and said, "Funny, you'd think Daley was smarter than that."

"What are you talking about?" Fineen asked.

"Swiping his old lady's money."

"Where'd you hear that?"

"Hear it? Hell, I didn't hear it, Fineen. I added two and two and got four." He turned inside the shop. "Come here. Want to show you something." He walked over to his bench and slapped a fine saddle tree. "I'm making this up for Bill Daley. Won't be anything like it in the county. Silver mountings and all." He winked. "Making him a harness too. Nigh onto six hundred dollars' worth of stuff." He poked Fineen in the chest. "After all these years, Bill found where she's hid the money. That's what she's mad about. I told Ab Larkin in the store, and he must have said something to Daley's wife."

A DULL alarm tolled in the back of Finley Fineen's mind, yet he moved forward with great caution. "Collins, you've been taken in. Daley won't ever pay for this stuff."

"Ha! He's already paid for it." The saddlemaker went to his cubbyhole desk. "Here. Paid cash." He flipped the bills under Fineen's nose.

A canker formed in Fineen's stomach and he found breathing difficult. He had to get out before Collins

170

saw his expression. Fineen turned to the door and walked rapidly down the street. Collins came out and stared after him, then shook his head and went back inside his shop.

Harness! Saddle! The son of a bitch probably bought horses too; this was Fineen's thought as he walked toward the livery stable. Sonnerman was pitching hay toward the back of the barn as Fineen walked through.

"I want to talk to you," Fineen said.

"Well, I ain't never too busy to do that," the old man said. "What's on your mind?"

"Did Bill Daley tell you to buy him a team?"

"You heard, huh?" Sonnerman chuckled. "I guess he found where she hid the money. He's spendin' it like a drunk Indian."

Fineen's expression was stricken; he knew where Daley got that money and panic crowded him. He forced himself to speak calmly. "Thanks," he said and walked out.

He controlled his urge to kill and compound an already fatal mistake on Daley's part. God, didn't the man understand that this was all it would take to hang them all? Of course he understood that the town would think Daley had found where Ethel had salted the money, and that was all right, because Fineen wasn't worried about the damned town. But Lincoln McKeever and that insurance detective wouldn't be fooled, not for a minute, and once the house started to collapse, it would be too late to run from under it.

I'll have to get to Daley; this was Fineen's thought as he went back up the street, cutting across to the drugstore. He took the side steps two at a time and pushed open the door without knocking.

Daley and his wife were battling in the parlor; she was shouting and flourishing a vase while Daley cringed away, his arms upraised to ward off the blow about to descend at any time.

Ethel Daley did not hear Fineen approach; he snatched the vase away from her before she knew anyone else was in the room.

"Shut your loud mouth and get out of here," Fineen said fiercely.

She turned shocked, round eyes on him, then backed up a step. "What—what do you mean, breaking into my house?"

"Go on, get out of here! Get out or I'll run you in for disturbing the peace."

"Daley, are you going to let him talk to me like that?"

"I hope he does lock you up," Daley said. "You've gone completely crazy!" He had a cut on his forehead and a smear of blood on his cheek; he dabbed at these with a handkerchief.

Fineen took her by the arm and propelled her toward the door. "I said to go and cool off. Don't come back for an hour, do you hear?"

"The idea, coming in here like this—all right, I'll go." She gave Bill Daley a last look. "But I'm not through with you, you sneak!"

"Yes, you're through," Fineen snapped and slammed the outside door, locking it so she could not come in unexpectedly.

Daley was kicking at some of the mess. "Sure glad you got here, Finley. Jesus, I don't know what got into the woman, I honestly don't. I was sitting here when she came busting in, raving mad."

"We'd better have a talk," Fineen said. "A real honest one, Bill."

"Honest?" Bill Daley stared at Fineen. "Man, we've always been honest with each other." He shook his head. "I'm going to have that woman put away, damned if I ain't. Crazy, that's what she is. Money crazy."

"What the hell else is there for her, married to a dried-up little prune like you."

"Huh? Finley, you had no call to say that. I thought we were friends."

"My friends are on the level with me," Fineen said. "You little runt, did you think you could get away with it? How dumb do you think I am, anyway?"

"Get away with what? Finley, for God's sake won't someone tell me what I done wrong instead of just cussing me out?"

"Don't stand there and play innocent with me," Fineen said. "It's all over town by now, the way you threw money around; clothes, new harness, horses; God, did you try to spend it all in one day?"

"Suits, harness? Finley, you're not making sense!"

"I'm not?" He hit Daley then, smashing him back into a chair. "Getting ready to run out on me, Bill? Leave me all alone to face McKeever, is that it?"

Unmindful of his bleeding nose, Daley said, "I swear to all that's holy, Finley, I don't know what

173

you're talking about!"

"Aw, shut your lying mouth, you worthless little punk! I never wanted you in on this in the first place, you know that. You've got paper guts, that's what you got. McKeever scares you too easy."

Bill Daley acted like a man near tears, frustrated tears. "Finley, I'm telling you the truth. I never spent a nickel of that money. Not one nickel."

"You're a liar! You scattered it all over town!"

"Would I be that dumb? Would I? Ah, Finley, listen to me, will you?"

"You're pretty dumb and you're scared," Fineen said. "Sorry, Bill, but I can't afford to listen to you now. McKeever's breathing too close down my neck now. I can't take a chance with you."

"Wha—what're you going to do? Finley, think about this now. Don't do anything hasty now."

"I won't," Fineen said. "You think I'll shoot you here?" He shook his head. "No, I'm too smart for that. It gets dark every night, Bill, and when it gets dark enough, I might take a shot at you. So you watch yourself, huh? And don't go near McKeever or that San Francisco investigator. One word to him and you're a dead man, because wherever you are, I won't be out of shooting range. Just remember that."

BILL Daley's fear was genuine. "Finley, in the name of God, trust me! I'm not a bad man. You've known me for years; I've never done anything wrong."

"I guess you believe that," Fineen said softly. "Maybe we all believe that, you, me, and Wade. You might call that our biggest mistake, trying to go on, respectable, when we killed and stole."

"You're not making sense," Daley said.

"Yes I am. If you're going to be bad, Bill, then be bad all the way. I mean, know you're bad. The trouble with us is that we don't believe we're no good, when really we're as rotten as ever were born."

"I've tried to live right, Finley! You know I have. Hell, before this, I never did anything wrong. Please, Finley, believe me now."

"Too late," Fineen said. "Way too late, Bill."

"All right," Daley said, angry at last. "All right, you loud-mouth, if that's the way you want it. You'd better shoot me now because as soon as you leave I'm going to McKeever and spill my guts. You think I want to worry and watch the rest of my life? By God I'd like one decent night's sleep before I die." He smiled then, his manner cocky. "Go ahead and shoot me, big brains. That shot will bring the town on the run and you'll hang because there isn't a lie in the world big enough to cover for you now." He got up from the floor and brushed his clothes briefly. "I'm going to be generous with you, Finley. Real generous. I'm going to give you some time, say a half hour, to clear out of Two Pines alive."

Finley Fineen pulled his gun and cocked it, then he stood there, thinking this over. He understood the truth of Daley's statement: pull the trigger and he'd be as good as dead. Go, and he had a half hour, which was better than nothing. Still, there was another way, and he tried it.

"I lost my temper, Bill. Hell, if we don't break and run, McKeever can't pin a thing on either of us." He tried a smile, the old friendly smile. "How about it, Bill? Friends?"

"No," Daley said. "Stop fooling yourself, Finley. McKeever will never give up until he's got us. Take the half hour and be thankful for it."

Finley Fineen slowly uncocked his gun and put it away. "Bill, what the hell happened to us? We were going to hold the money for five years. Sit back, safe, while McKeever ground his nose into the ground trying to figure it out." He shook his head. "We did everything right, the shell, the damned gun, everything right."

"No," Daley said. "We did everything wrong, Finley. We robbed a man, and killed him. No matter what else was right, that was wrong enough to wipe out everything else."

"None of us really needed the money," Fineen said, as though he were trying to justify himself. "A man's just got to do something once in a while that ain't been done before. You know that's a fact, Bill. Why can't we face McKeever out? It'll work, I tell you!"

"It won't work," Daley said. "Maybe some other kind of a man could make it work, but not us, Finley." He nodded toward the door. "You'd better get going."

"God, I've got a wife, a business!"

"Finley, you don't have a damn thing except a sackful of money. I hope you enjoy it, wherever you stop long enough to spend it. But you won't stop much. You won't dare. In a half a year's time your neck will have a permanent crink in it from looking over your shoulder." He stood there a moment, then crossed to the door and unlocked it. "I'll start counting when you get to the bottom of the stairs."

"Jesus—" Then Finley Fineen closed his mouth.

"It's a poor way for a man to end, isn't it, Finley?"

Fineen stopped on the stairs and looked briefly. "Yes," he said. "Bill, I've got nothing against you. It was meant to work out this way, I guess."

"It would have worked as you planned," Daley said, "if we'd been more like Wade."

Fineen frowned. "I've thought that, but then, he's dead, isn't he?" He turned then and hurried down to the street. At the bottom of the steps he met Ethel Daley, and he spoke to her briefly. She looked up at her husband, then came up the stairs, running, crying.

"Come on inside," he said softly. "I've got something to tell you, Ethel."

18.

LINCOLN McKEEVER WAS PEELING THE WRAPPER from a cigar when Finley Fineen came down the stairway; Boomhauer's nudge raised his attention. They watched Fineen speak briefly to Ethel Daley, then when Fineen hurried to his office, Boomhauer said, "What do you think, Lincoln? Has he nibbled at the bait?"

"A little early to tell," McKeever said. "If we move a bit too fast now we'll lose it all."

"Yes, and if we poke around, we may still lose."

"That's a chance we have to take," McKeever said. "Want to finish the game?"

"Not for a while," Boomhauer said. He saw Jim Singleton come out on the porch across the street and signaled him. When Jim came across the street, Boomhauer said, "Will you sort of keep an eye on Finley Fineen? Stay out of sight as much as you can though. I just want to know what he's up to."

"All right," Jim said and walked on down the street.

McKeever's cigar was about done for when Ethel Daley came slowly down the stairs. She looked up and down the street before she saw McKeever, and when she raised her hand, he stepped off the saloon porch and walked toward her, Charlie Boomhauer tagging along a pace behind.

There is little attractiveness left in a woman when she has been crying, but Ethel Daley no longer cared how she looked. She spoke to Lincoln McKeever. "Bill's upstairs. He killed Doc Harris."

McKeever's glance touched Boomhauer briefly. "I'll go," Boomhauer said.

Not wanting to draw a crowd, McKeever walked Ethel Daley to the hotel. He steered her into Nan's room without a word, then closed the door. Nan came in from the kitchen and McKeever said, "If you have some coffee on, I think Mrs. Daley would like some."

"Something wrong, Lincoln?"

"Not now," he said. "Just bring some coffee."

"He told me what he did," Ethel said. "I can't believe it. I just can't."

"You'll have to believe it," McKeever said gently. "Bill went off the deep end, that's all. A man sometimes does that."

Nan came back with a tray; there was no more talk until Mrs. Daley had a cup in her hands. "There were three of them, Fineen, Bill, and Wade Stanton. Fineen killed Dalridge. Bill killed poor Doc because he got scared." Her eyes were dull and slow moving. "I just can't believe my Bill would do a thing like that. He's always been such a gentle man, Sheriff."

"I'm not the sheriff," McKeever said.

"It was you he was afraid of," she said. "He told me that."

Nan said, "Lincoln, did Bill Daley confess—"

He waved her silent. "Mrs. Daley, you know what's going to happen don't you?"

"I guess you'll hang him," she said. "He was never a mean man." She looked steadily at McKeever. "I loved him, did you know that? But I never did right by him. I wanted to, but somehow I was always so afraid."

"Of what?"

She shrugged. "Losing him, I guess. I was never a pretty woman, you see. Sweet, everybody said, but awful dowdy. Catching a man can be hard when you're something everybody looks through instead of looking at. Poor Bill, he just couldn't make up his mind, even after we went together for three years. I guess I pushed him into marrying me. A man resents a thing like that, you know. A woman's got to give a man freedom if she wants to hold him. I wanted to be

179

that way, but I just couldn't. You fight for something and you want to hold tight to it. Poor Bill, I guess I just choked all the manhood out of him." She paused to drink some of her coffee; McKeever and Nan exchanged glances. "I never should have got on him like I did, after him all the time, taking all his money, but I had to. Some don't know what it is to be afraid, and I was scared I'd lose him to another woman. Mr. McKeever, you've got to understand that to some, hate is as good as love; at least it's something." She shook her head slowly. "I guess I was going to lose him anyway, him spending all that stolen money the way he did. That's what brought it on. He was fixing to leave me and I couldn't help getting mad. You can understand that, can't you, Mr. McKeever?"

"Bill wasn't going to leave you," McKeever said. "You see, I spent that money for him. Me and Mr. Boomhauer."

She stared at him. "You did? Now you've got me all mixed up. You knew my Bill had robbed Mr. Dalridge?"

"I knew it but I couldn't prove it," McKeever said. He did not bother to explain to her; he wasn't sure she was in any condition to understand if he did explain. "Nan, will you take care of her? See if you can get her to lie down and rest."

"All right, Lincoln."

He stepped outside just as Charlie Boomhauer came into the lobby. "I got him in jail," Boomhauer said. "I also notified Kelly and Burgess; they're coming right in." Boomhauer took off his hat and mopped away the sweat trapped there. "He made a full confession. I think we can arrest Fineen now and make it stick."

"Did you recover the money?"

BOOMHAUER took it out of an inner pocket and made a brief fan of it before putting it back. "Eighteen thousand."

McKeever whistled softly. "Didn't Kelly and Burgess claim around forty apiece?"

"They were lying," Boomhauer said, then smiled. "But that's not unusual when trying to collect from an insurance company. I know where Stanton hid his money too."

"The hell? Did Daley know?"

"Yes," Boomhauer said. "They even worked out the individual hiding places, sort of a test to determine whether it was foolproof or not. Stanton buried his share under the manure pile. I'll have a crew go out there and dig it up as soon as Mrs. Stanton pays off the hands and leaves." He clapped both hands over his breast pockets. "Got a cigar? I'm out."

McKeever offered him one, and a match. "Did Daley say where Fineen was?"

"No," Boomhauer said. "But the man can't be far." He squinted through a haze of smoke. "We've got to get that damned badge off of him. I'll speak to Kelly and Burgess about it as soon as they get to town."

"You want to go over to Fineen's house with me, Charlie?"

"Yes, I think I will." He turned to the street with McKeever. As they walked along, Boomhauer said,

"Funny thing about Daley. He talked about Stanton, but not about Fineen."

"Didn't he tell you Finley hid his share of the money?"

"No," Boomhauer said. "And I didn't press him too hard. We'll find that out when we pick up Fineen." He smiled. "I don't think he'll get far with Jim watching him."

Madge Fineen was in the back yard, hanging up the week's washing. When no one answered the front door, Lincoln McKeever let himself in. Then they went to the back porch; Mrs. Fineen seemed surprised to see them coming out the back door.

"Well, do you always walk through a body's house?"

"No," McKeever said. "Where's Finley?"

"How would I know. I hardly seem him anymore, with his sheriff's duties and all."

"Would you come in the house a minute?" McKeever asked.

Madge Fineen frowned. "I've my washing to do."

"You'd better come in," Charlie Boomhauer said, and something in his voice made her put the bag of clothespins down.

She wiped her hands on her apron and went ahead of them into the house. "If you're expecting me to fix coffee, you're mistaken. This is my busiest day."

"No thanks," McKeever said softly. "Will you sit down, please?"

"I like standing," she said. "Get on with it. I said I was busy."

McKeever was suddenly without words to tell this woman what he had to tell her. Charlie Boomhauer said, "Mrs. Fineen, we're going to have to arrest your husband."

She seemed indignant. "For what? You don't have the authority."

"I'm afraid we have," Boomhauer said. "Won't you please sit down now?" When she settled in a kitchen chair, Boomhauer told her of the charges, mentioning Bill Daley's arrest and confession. Listening to this man talk, Lincoln McKeever learned the power of a persuasive voice, a commanding manner. Boomhauer always spoke softly, yet with finality, with rock-steady assurance; people didn't often argue with him.

MADGE Fineen listened, her lip caught between her teeth. There were tears to be shed, but she held them back. Finally she said, "I knew he was a bothered man of late. Not able to sleep good, and he didn't eat his meals like he should." She turned her head to stare out the window. "My Finley with blood on his hands?" She pressed her fingers against her mouth. "My Finley. I bore him three children, you know. One died at birth, and two before they could walk. Lung fever. But he never blamed me, not my Finley. I love the man."

"We want you to stay home," McKeever said. "Finley's around town somewhere and we have to go after him. If you want, I'll send someone to stay with you."

She shook her head. "I just want to be alone."

"Are you sure you'll be all right?" Boomhauer asked.

She turned her head slowly and stared at him. "All right? Do you think anything will ever be all right again? God, why did he do it? We were happy, Finley and me. Oh, there were things we both wanted and could never have, but there's always something someone wants that they can never have."

I guess Finley wanted some things you didn't know about," McKeever said. His nod brought Boomhauer along and they went out the front door.

"That's always a dirty job," Boomhauer said. "Telling some innocent person about a thing like that."

"Don't you get toughened up to it?"

"No," Boomhauer said. "Somehow you never do. At least, I never did."

By the time they reached the main street, the whole town knew about Bill Daley and Finley Fineen. They even understood why Wade Stanton drew against McKeever's drop, and in their way, they forgave McKeever without taking back all the things they had thought about McKeever and Betty Stanton.

Burgess and Kelly stormed into town in their buggy and stopped by McKeever and. Boomhauer. "My God, what a shocking development," Kelly said as he dismounted. Burgess tied the horse, then wiped sweat from his face.

"To think we appointed Fineen sheriff," Burgess said. "Well, that's a mistake that will soon be corrected."

"Yes," Boomhauer said smoothly. "And while

you're at it, gentlemen, I would also go over your claims again to make sure the amount filed is absolutely correct." He waited while both men glanced at each other. "A good deal of the money has been recovered and we expect to get the rest of it shortly. I'm sure you understand."

"Ah—yes," Olin Kelly said. "We did check, Mr. Boomhauer, and I'm happy to say that the amount is considerably less."

"Fine," Boomhauer said, smiling. "A little less profit in it for you, perhaps, but it makes for better relations between the home office and the insured."

Jim Singleton came rushing down the street and rudely pushed his way through a thin rank of onlookers. "Lincoln, Fineen's skipped out!"

"What? You're sure?"

"Hell, he saddled a horse and rode out five or ten minutes ago. Heading north."

"Go saddle my bay, and get a horse for Boomhauer."

"My interest is mainly money right now," Boomhauer said, "not that I wouldn't enjoy a man-hunt. I'll leave Fineen to you, McKeever. Just make sure you get him."

"I'll damn sure get him," McKeever said. "Go on, Jim. Get that horse saddled."

McKEEVER excused himself and walked across to the Hanover House. Nan was in the kitchen and she seemed surprised to see him. "Trouble at Fineen's?"

"If I hadn't been so damned busy congratulating myself on how smart I am," McKeever said, "I'd have guessed that Bill Daley bought his life from Fineen for a head start." He took a flour sack and began to fill it with staples.

"You're going after him?"

"What else? He's got eighteen thousand dollars that doesn't belong to him and an appointment with a rope."

"Better take a skillet along." Then she took the sack away from him. "Here, let me do that. Go have a cigar and calm down. Fineen isn't that much ahead."

"If he gets into those mountains to the north, an hour is all he'll need." He walked up and down the kitchen a few times, then paused to look out the back door. "I should have gone after Fineen as soon as Daley confessed. And I keep asking myself why I didn't. Hell, I'm not afraid of the man!"

"Here's your sack," Nan said.

He took it from her. "Is that all you have to say?"

"Well, what do you want me to say?"

"You're not that dumb," he said and took her into his arms. She raised her lips for his kiss and he held her that way for a long moment. When he released her, he asked, "Satisfied?"

She was on the edge of a smile. "Should I be?"

"You made me come to you," he said. "Isn't that what you wanted?"

"Yes," she said. "Now I'll never pick at you again."

Jim came running through the hotel. He smiled when Nan quickly disengaged herself from McKeever's arms. "The horses are saddled and waiting, Lincoln."

186

"You can take one back," McKeever said, shouldering the sack. "Boomhauer's not going."

"But I am," Jim said flatly.

"You are not!" Nan said. Then she looked at McKeever, and back to her brother, and a smile raised the ends of her lips. "Pa's .45 is in the drawer behind the counter. But be careful."

With a whoop Jim Singleton ran to get it. McKeever said, "Nan, he'll thank you for that."

"No he won't," she said. "But I guess you were right, Lincoln. The time's come."

19.

THE EASY WAY WOULD HAVE BEEN TO TELEGRAPH ahead and have the law waiting for Finley Fineen, but Lincoln McKeever wasn't about to take the easy way. Not this time. He would run Fineen down and bring him back kicking and yelling for the town to look at.

With Jim Singleton at his side, McKeever pushed north, following the game trails and clinging always to the high ground that afforded him the best view. This was a land of lodge pine and underbrush, and rock outcroppings, and his direction often seemed confused, yet McKeever knew where he was going. A few years of working these woods as a logger had sharpened his sense of direction, and at the end of the day, he was miles ahead of where he would have been if he had followed the road.

From the eagle's nest ridge, McKeever stopped to look out across a broad, grassed valley. "He's down there somewhere," McKeever said, pointing. Darkness was not far away, and in the valley a twilight was already falling. The distant gleam of lights marked a solitary place, while a few miles beyond the road arched upward to cross a timbered ridge.

"If he's down there," Jim Singleton said, "then what're we doing up here?"

McKeever laughed. "Don't you like it up here, Jim?" He nodded toward the lights. "I'll lay you odds that Finley's sitting down to supper there, or at best, he's just finished eating and is getting ready to leave." McKeever's glance went on to the far ridge. "About midnight, Finley'll top that. If he keeps on going, he'll be in the clear."

"It's fifty-five miles to the nearest town," Jim said. "And he wouldn't head there, Lincoln."

"Wouldn't he?" McKeever shook his head. "He has to, Jim. There's a railroad there. Finley's a town man, Jim. He'll stick to the roads and bluff or fight his way through if he has to. And he'll head for a railroad to catch a train East." He jigged his horse into motion. "Come on. I'd like to be waiting in the depot when Finley goes to buy his ticket."

"Hell, we'll have to ride all night to get ahead of him."

"So, we'll ride all night," McKeever said.

During the long hours, the tiring hours, he told himself that he was being a fool about this; how much easier it would have been to wire ahead for a reception committee. But there were certain things that a man had to do alone, and McKeever felt that this was one of them. With a stranger, he might have felt differently, but not Finley Fineen, a man he had known for years. When you've called a man friend, like he had, the personal contact always remained, even up to the scaffold.

Jim Singleton's determination to be a good deputy sheriff overcame his weariness. He offered no complaint at the long hours McKeever put in the saddle, the aching miles traveled, or the briefness of the stops McKeever made.

At a quarter after three, Lincoln McKeever held the face of his watch close to his eyes to read the hands. "We've passed him," he said, the first words he had spoken in hours.

"You sound damn sure," Jim said softly.

"Finley's a buggy man," McKeever said. "Been four or five years since he's ridden astraddle. We've passed him."

"Then we can take it easier, huh?"

McKeever laughed. "When you're chasing a man, Jim, you never take it easy. Especially when you want to come back alive."

He mounted again and Jim Singleton wearily pulled himself into the saddle. They did not stop again until dawn, and only then to watch the sun's first rays make silver cords of a pair of railroad rails trailing off to the faintest horizons.

The town of Buffalo lay ahead and they began to cut

off the last of the high ground, angling down to the basin floor. An hour later they met the road and went on into town. Buffalo was larger than Two Pines, a cattle town with a cattleman's indifference to cleanliness and careful planning. McKeever counted eight saloons in three blocks and this alone marked it as cattle bought and paid for.

The depot lay on the south end, but instead of going directly there, McKeever rode down a quiet side street and dismounted to tie his horse.

Jim said, "Wouldn't the stable be better?"

"Finley might go there. I wouldn't want him to recognize our horses."

"If he's so eager to get out of town, he'll go straight to the depot."

"Still I don't want to take the chance," McKeever said. "Feel up to a cup of coffee, Jim?"

"Man, I could do with the pot."

They tried two restaurants and found them closed, but the saloon was open and the bartender was brewing himself some coffee. McKeever placed his hat on the bar and said, "A bottle, one glass, and two cups of that coffee."

While the bartender served up, his glance took in their dusty clothes, and the haggard expression both wore around the eyes. "Been movin' some, ain't you?"

"Considerable," McKeever admitted. He tasted the coffee, then smiled. "Man, you are a genius with the brown bean." He nudged Jim Singleton. "Good, huh?"

"Sure is."

"When do the trains run around here?" McKeever asked.

"Depends on where you're going. There's an eastbound due in around one this afternoon."

McKeever poured a glass of whisky for himself, then shoved the bottle away from him. His glance found the wall clock briefly: twenty minutes after six.

"There's a town ordinance about carrying firearms in the city limits," the bartender said, glancing at their guns. "Just thought I'd tell you that to spare you any trouble."

"I appreciate it," McKeever said.

The bartender waited, then said, "You can check 'em here if you want."

"Ah—maybe later," McKeever said. He finished his coffee, then nudged Jim again. "Let's walk around."

"Fellas, the marshal's pretty strict about the no gun law."

"Thank you. We'll remember that," McKeever said and pushed aside the swinging doors.

They paused on the boardwalk a moment to scan the street. Jim said, "Where do you plan to take him, Lincoln?"

"Where no one will get hurt in case he starts shooting," McKeever said.

"Catch him on the outskirts of town," Jim suggested. "That way we wouldn't have to worry about that marshal and his no gun law."

"Yeah," McKeever said, brushing his beard stubble. "The trouble with that is that a man is just naturally wide awake when he rides into a strange town. It appears to me that we wouldn't surprise Finley much by jumping him too quick." He shook his head. "No, I'd like to give Finley a chance to get a drink and drop his guard a little. Let's go on down to the depot. We'll wait there."

"How long do you figure?" Jim asked.

"Three hours, maybe four." McKeever looked at him carefully. "Getting jumpy?"

"Some. I never been in this kind of a spot before."

"Well, don't feel bad. A man always gets jumpy at a time like this."

"Yeah? You don't act that way."

"How I act," McKeever said, "and how I feel are two different things." He put his hand briefly on Jim Singleton's shoulder. "I hope you never have to shoot a man, Jim. But if you do, I hope the decision comes quick, in a matter of seconds, when it's draw or die. I don't want you to ever have to know beforehand that killing will be necessary, like I did when I faced Wade Stanton." He let his eyes run up and down the street again. "That way is always bad, Jim. Bad because you have to think about it, before, as well as afterward."

"Stanton was a guilty man," Jim said. "It makes a difference when he's guilty."

"Does it?"

"Sure it does."

"Someday you may find out different," McKeever said. "Come on, let's go down to the depot."

A STATION agent was wrestling baggage when Mc-

Keever and Singleton walked in and sat down on one of the benches near the front where they could see the street approach. The agent came in, peered at them, then said, "Train ain't due for hours yet."

"We'll wait," McKeever said.

An hour earlier, Jim Singleton had thought of nothing but sleep, now he found it out of the question; he could never remember feeling so alert, so fine-tuned.

"I've been thinking," he said. "You know, about Finley and the others, and what made them rob Dalridge." He shifted, trying to find a nonexistent soft spot on the hard bench. "Lincoln, to tell you the truth, I've felt like doing something crazy. It seems like there's nothing for a fella to do in Two Pines, except hang around and wait to grow up." He grew thoughtful for a moment. "Lincoln, sometimes it's a terrible thing to grow up in a town where everybody knows you. After a time they don't pay any attention to you, or even look at you. Hell, I've had the notion to take a gun and shoot out a half a dozen store windows just so people would look at me."

"But you never did," McKeever said.

"Yeah, I never did. But I thought about it." He looked at McKeever quickly. "Do you suppose that's how it started? I mean, one of them said, 'What this town needs is a damned good holdup.'"

"Probably," McKeever said. "That would be Stanton talking, Jim. He was that way, quick to find fault, the first to object; the man liked trouble, deep down inside, only it takes more than a liking for trouble to be a real badman, Jim. Wade Stanton didn't have that."

"You think Fineen has?"

"Yes," McKeever said quickly. "I think he has, but he don't know it yet. And I want to get him before he finds out."

"I don't follow you."

"Well, let's take Wade first. He came after me, face to face, but he didn't want it that way. Pride pushed him, and that liking for trouble. I think Wade expected me to back down. Bill Daley? Yes, he killed Doc Harris, but out of fright and desperation. He fought because he was cornered, nothing else. Whether he actually was or not is not important. What is important is that he *thought* he was cornered."

"And Finley?"

"He killed Dalridge because he enjoyed it. Jim, a man would have to enjoy deliberately clubbing a man to death to do so thorough a job. We all have a sleeping rage in us, Jim. You felt it when you had the urge to shoot out some windows. Finley Fineen had it when he clubbed Dalridge to death with his gun barrel. So when you find a man who lets that rage loose on the world you have a killer, without conscience or hesitation. A man like Finley."

JIM Singleton tapped McKeever on the shoulder, drawing his attention to the street fronting the depot. McKeever saw the badge first, the man second. Then the marshal stepped into the depot and took a quick left and right look. He came over and said, "Howdy, gents. Passing through?"

"Yes," McKeever said.

The marshal pursed his full lips and brushed his mustache with his forefinger. "Sorry to trouble you, but we have an ordnance about sidearms. Like to have you check them with the station agent until you leave."

"We won't leave the depot," McKeever said. "Can't you alter the rules a little this time?"

"Afraid not," the marshal said. "Rules aren't meant to be altered in this town." He held out his hand. "I'll check 'em for you and save you the trouble."

Watching this man, Lincoln McKeever saw that he wasn't bucking some soft-headed town loafer wearing a badge. The marshal was a relaxed, easy-mannered man, who always kept his right hand at his side, not too far from a well-worn Smith & Wesson .44.

"My name is Lincoln McKeever, the sheriff from Two Pines. This is my deputy, Jim Singleton."

"Oh? Then I guess you got some kind of identification, a badge maybe?"

"No, I don't," McKeever said. "I expect you'll just have to take my word for it."

"I can't do that," the marshal said. "Let's have the guns or we'll go over to the jail."

Lincoln McKeever cursed this man beneath his breath, yet he held no genuine anger against him; he would have done exactly the same thing in Two Pines. "All right," he said. "Give him your gun, Jim."

Unbuckling his belt, Jim Singleton rolled it around the holster and handed it to the marshal; McKeever was tugging at his own buckle, then it came loose and started to slip to the floor. He made a frantic grab for it, but missed and let it fall. The marshal grunted in surprise as he looked into the bore of McKeever's pistol.

"You learn a new trick every day," the marshal said bitterly.

"Put your gun back on," McKeever said, and when Jim Singleton refastened the belt, he said, "Now take the marshal over to the bench and see that he sets down. Cover him but don't let your gun show." He picked his own gunbelt up off the floor and put it on, holstering his pistol.

McKeever and Jim Singleton sandwiched the town marshal between them and Jim kept the muzzle of his .45 pressed into the marshal's side.

"Now I'm sure sorry we have to do it this way," McKeever said softly, "but I wasn't lying about being the sheriff. There's a man coming here, or at least I guess he'll head here, and I mean to arrest him. Now you're going to sit right there with Jim's gun on you while I take this guy. Afterward, if you want to ease your mind, you can telegraph Two Pines and confirm my story. But right now you're doing to behave yourself, understand?"

"I understand," the marshal said. "But boy, you'd better be telling me this straight. If you ain't, I'll see that you spend a year in jail." He looked at Jim Singleton. "That goes for you too, Billy the Kid."

"That's enough talk," McKeever said softly. "Just be comfortable and act like an old friend, huh?"

196

20.

A T TEN O'CLOCK LINCOLN MCKEEVER'S WORRY
began to grow to alarming proportions and he
kept his attention on the road leading to the depot. Jim
was getting tired of holding the gun and the marshal
was getting tired of sitting so long.

He said, "Your bluff won't work, McKeever. If you
think you can hold me here until train time, then get
away, you're crazy. I'll telegraph ahead and have you
taken off and brought back."

"We're not getting on the train," McKeever said.

"Where the hell can he be?" Jim Singleton asked.
"Lincoln, you suppose you guessed wrong?"

"No, I don't think so. This is Finley's best chance, if
he ever gets here."

When twelve o'clock came, Lincoln McKeever
would have given five dollars for a cup of coffee and
a plate of stew. In the back room the station agent
cooked his dinner and the aroma was maddening. The
marshal sat quietly, looking at each of them from time
to time. "What you done?"

"Huh?" McKeever asked, his attention pulled
around.

"I said, what was it? Holdup? A shooting?"

"You're out of your mind," McKeever said. "Just
shut up and sit still."

The station clock ticked loudly, monotonously, and
a lazy heat filled the place. Not many people came to

the depot for it was a short distance from the center of town, and McKeever was thankful for that small favor.

At one o'clock the station agent began to wheel freight onto the cinder platform, and in the distance, a train whistle hooted for a crossing. The town marshal said, "Not much time left, boys."

"I told you to shut up," McKeever said. He pulled his lips tight and looked out the window. "Where the hell can he be? Was I wrong?"

"If you were," Jim said, "we'll never catch him with this much head start."

"I wasn't wrong!" McKeever said tightly. "Damn it, I can't be! I know Finley too well. He'd think of the train. He's just not a man who likes to ride, especially when he has a lot of miles to cover."

"Train'll be here in ten minutes," the marshal said. "If you want to put that gun away, sonny, I'll see that you get off light, say only ninety days."

"We'll play this McKeever's way," Jim Singleton said.

They sat there while the train drew nearer, finally clanking into the station where it sighed to a halt. A few passengers got down and the baggage car door opened to take on freight. McKeever watched this activity with a maddening sense of defeat.

"Lincoln!" Jim's tone was enough; McKeever looked out the window.

FINLEY Fineen was cutting across the street, his step rapid. He had a pair of saddlebags over his left arm and his pistol was riding on the front of his thigh, where it would be handy.

With a start, McKeever saw what Fineen's plan was, and he hurriedly stood up. "Keep the marshal here, Jim," he said and ran for the back door of the depot. The ticket clerk tried to block him and McKeever knocked him asprawl, then charged onto the platform. Fineen intended to board the train without a ticket, buying it from the conductor, then if anyone found out how he had escaped, they would have a tougher time tracing his destination.

Finley Fineen had his foot on the coach step when McKeever ran clear of the building. He said, "That's far enough, Finley!"

For a heartbeat Fineen hesitated, statue-still, his hands raised to the grabrail. Then he whirled, drawing his gun, and McKeever's hand plucked his own pistol free of the holster. He had a slight edge on Fineen, and shot first, but Fineen had the saddlebags before him, chest high, and McKeever saw the bullet bury in the money.

Fineen's bullet snapped at the brim of his hat, then McKeever rolled his thumb across the hammer again, this time shooting a little lower. Fineen grunted as the bullet took him in the stomach and fell back against the coach. He tried to work his gun, but his strength was draining away. Finally he let his gun fall, and followed it ungracefully.

Going forward, McKeever picked up the saddle-bags, then rolled Finley Fineen over with his foot. Heads lined the raised coach windows, then the conductor signaled the engineer and the train panted into motion drawing clear of the station.

Jim Singleton came out then, still covering the town marshal. He looked at Fineen, then said, "You're a good guesser, Lincoln."

"Yep," McKeever said. "But he had me damned worried."

The marshal said, "Say, you really were after this fella, weren't you?"

"You're getting the idea," McKeever said. He began to unbuckle the saddlebag. "There's about twelve thousand dollars in stolen money in here." He showed the marshal, who whistled softly. "Have you got a safe where I can put this?"

"Sure."

"My deputy and I are going to get a meal, a bath, and a shave," McKeever said. "Tonight, I'd like to get fresh horses for the trip back to Two Pines." He smiled. "And that'll give you time to check on us by telegraph."

"I don't guess that's necessary now," the marshal said. "But you two ought to carry some kind of identification on you."

"After this," McKeever said, "we will. Come on, Jim. You'll take care of this?"

"Sure," the marshal said. "I'll lock this saddlebag up right away." He looked again at Fineen. "He'll draw a crowd—hey, Fred, loan me one of your freight carts to pack this fella over to the jail."

FIVE hours' sleep, a bath, a good meal and a shave

can change a man's outlook on life; at least it did for Lincoln McKeever. He was not sorry that Fineen chose to shoot it out; in fact he rather expected it. Somehow the thought of taking Finley Fineen back and hanging him in front of all the people who knew him left McKeever with a bad taste.

A bullet was quick, and dying in a strange town with no one to care could be a blessing in disguise.

That evening, with fresh horses and Fineen tied across one, McKeever got his saddlebags full of money from the town marshal, woke Jim Singleton from a sound sleep, and left town twenty minutes later.

They made an all night ride of it; McKeever liked night for traveling, and in the morning they stopped to brew a pot of coffee and cook a meal. When the fire was dirt-covered, McKeever motioned Jim Singleton into the saddle, and drew a mild complaint.

McKeever stayed on the road going back, but he didn't stop often, or for long, and by his manner, Jim Singleton could draw some definite conclusions about this man, the sure way he had of doing everything.

Two Pines welcomed McKeever and Jim Singleton as a couple of heroes, and McKeever was somewhat concerned about how Jim would react to this sudden acclaim. But the young man shrugged it off, put up the horses, then went home. Finley Fineen was taken to his home; McKeever made no statement to Fineen's wife; he left her alone to do her crying.

Charlie Boomhauer was waiting for him at the jail. He took the saddlebag, counted the money briefly, then dumped it into the bottom desk drawer.

"I got the money back from the merchants," he said. "The company will return it to Kelly and Burgess within a few days; I've wired the home office for instructions." He looked at McKeever. "You look tired."

"Not the kind that sleep will cure," McKeever said. "The town's pretty keyed up, now that it's over. Bill Daley say anything more?"

"Yes, I have his statement, all the details. How Fineen made the gun and Daley the shell." He shook his head. "Lincoln, have you ever sat down and figured out how close these three came to getting away with this? I tell you, it was nearly the perfect crime."

"Except that they got caught."

"If it hadn't been for you, they wouldn't have," Boomhauer said.

"There's always someone like me around," McKeever said. "I hope that didn't sound like a brag."

"It didn't; I know how you meant it." Boomhauer took two cigars from his pocket and offered one to McKeever. "The home office is going to be damned pleased. They might offer you a remuneration."

"I don't want it," McKeever said.

"Don't be a damn fool, Lincoln. Take it." He waved his hands briefly. "I know how you feel. This is your town and you knew these men, but you can't think of that and you know it."

"Yeah," McKeever said. "A lawman is supposed to be hard, isn't he?"

"It sometimes helps," Boomhauer admitted. "I wish

I was." He nodded toward the cell blocks. "Daley wanted to see you as soon as you got back."

"All right, but I'm going over to the hotel first."

Boomhauer grinned. "A nice looking girl. I don't understand why you waited so long."

"Because I'm a fool," McKeever said and went out.

He had difficulty getting through the crowd milling up and down the street; they wanted to shake hands and tell him how good he was, and McKeever didn't want to listen to it.

He found Nan in her room; she answered the door quickly. "Jim came home ten minutes ago. I wondered if you'd come here, Lincoln."

"There's no place else I want to go," he said.

She motioned him into a chair, then sat on the arm. "I know you had to kill Finley, and I'm sorry. But it was better than hanging him, Lincoln."

"Yes. I don't want to hang Daley; I wish someone would do it."

"His trial begins Monday," she said. "I suppose it'll be a formality." She fell silent a moment. "I feel sorry for his wife; she'll have to live with this, like dirt that won't wash off."

"I'm going to resign," McKeever said. "All the way back from Buffalo I thought about it. I've got some money saved. Maybe I can find a business that suits me, somewhere away from here."

"Do you really want to leave here?"

He shrugged. "The town's kind of wore out for me, Nan. You know what I mean?"

"Yes. We all feel that way from time to time. You know, there have been times in my life when I've thought of running away with a gambler or a whisky drummer just to be doing it. Twenty years from now people would remember me and shake their heads sadly, yet they'd remember."

He looked at her quickly, his eyes serious. "Why did you tell me that?"

"Because we all see ourselves as being different from what we really are, I guess. I don't think many of us really like what we are, yet we have to go on living with it." She got up from the chair arm and moved around. "Idiots are contented, Lincoln. We're all restless and wandering, even if it's only in thought. After we're married, I'll feel the same way, and I want you to understand it, just as I intend to understand you."

He stood up, hat in hand. "I love you, Nan. It's been a long time since I said that."

"Yes, but it still sounds wonderful." She put her arms around him and kissed him briefly. "Go on now. When this is all over, we'll get married."

"Are we going to fight, Nan?"

"Sure," she said, smiling. "Do you want a wife or a freak?"

He was serious. "Nan, let's not grow tired of each other."

"I don't think we ever could," she said. "Now go on. Come back when you can."

He made his way to the jail; Boomhauer was still there, sitting on the company's money.

"You want the keys?" Boomhauer asked.

"I'm not going in the cell," McKeever said. He took off his gunbelt and laid it on the desk as a precaution against having it grabbed away from him.

Bill Daley occupied the center cell, away from the windows, in case some citizen decided to hurry justice with a rifle bullet. As McKeever stepped down the short hall, Daley came off the cot and pressed against the bars.

"You got him. I heard the noise in the street. They wouldn't yell and carry on like that if you hadn't got him." He looked around, his eyes wide and wildly rolling. "Well, where is he? Ain't you going to lock him up? He's as guilty as me. More so. He talked me into this. Yes, siree, I didn't want any part of it but Finley made me go along. He's the guilty one. I'm just an innocent man who got caught up in something he couldn't get out of. Come on now. You bring him in here and lock him up!"

"Finley's dead," McKeever said.

"Dead?" Daley stared. "You're lying to me, trying to scare me, that's what you're doing, Lincoln. Hell, I always liked you. We've been friends, haven't we? Good friends. Now you stop this lying to me and bring Fineen in here where he belongs."

"I'm not lying, Bill. Finley went for his gun and I had to kill him."

For a full minute Daley just stared and rubbed his face and shook his head, saying, "No, no, no, no."

"You're all alone, Bill. I'm sorry, but that's the way it turned out."

"Alone?" He grabbed the bars and tried to shake them. "I don't want to be alone!" Tears suddenly began to race down his cheeks and his face twisted like a tormented child's. "Don't hang me alone! God, don't make me hang alone! I don't want to be alone!"

McKeever turned and walked back to the office, shutting the door, yet the sounds of the pleading, the crying, came through. Charlie Boomhauer raised his head and his eyes were sad.

"I guess he knows now. Really knows and understands."

"Yes. It's too bad a man has to know."

"You going to stay on, as sheriff, I mean?"

McKeever frowned. "What makes you think I want to quit?"

"Because I've had some tough ones too, and I wanted to quit. We all do now and then."

McKeever sat down in one of the chairs. "No, I'll stay, Charlie. This is my town. Besides, I'm going to get married pretty soon." He let his smile start and grow. "A married man has no business being unemployed, has he?"

"Nope," Boomhauer said, rising. "Come on, I'll buy you a drink to that."

Center Point Publishing
600 Brooks Road ● PO Box 1
Thorndike ME 04986-0001 USA

(207) 568-3717

US & Canada:
1 800 929-9108